For Sonya, who has spent the last fifteen years showing me that anything is possible when you reach for the stars…

Praise for The Swindlers of Doom

"Jim Yelton has created an entertaining story with raggedly colorful characters. I found myself drawn in from the get-go. A recommended read!" – Meg Phillips Crespy, Author of *ZenKinky and the Art of (Not Finding) Love on the Internet*

"*THE SWINDLERS OF DOOM* is one of my favorite indie projects I've read in the last few years. I had a great time reading that. It touched on a lot of things I've always loved in Sci-Fi." – Van Allen Plexico, Author of *The Sentinels* series and Host of The White Rocket Podcast

MIDNIGHT ENTERTAINMENT LLC PROUDLY PRESENTS

the SWINDLERS of DOOM

15th Anniversary Edition

Written by

Jim Yelton

Featuring Artwork by

Eric Borchert & Steve Newton

Based on the Original Radio Drama first broadcast
on KOPN Radio's *Theatre of the Mind*

First Midnight Entertainment trade paperback printing March 2015

ISBN: 978-0-9797078-1-0

An Original Publication of
Midnight Entertainment LLC

All Letters and Inquiries can be sent to:
Midnight Entertainment LLC
138 Highway 124 North
Hallsville, MO 65255
www.midnight-entertainment.com

MIDNIGHT
ENTERTAINMENT
THE FUTURE OF ENTERTAINMENT BEGINS AT MIDNIGHT

Introduction:

A Journey into Development Hell (2007)

It is pointed out in the underappreciated John Carpenter mystical martial arts flick *Big Trouble in Little China* that the Chinese have a lot of hells. So do filmmakers and one of the most well-known is among the first you encounter along your journey from idea to completed film…Development Hell.

Development Hell has disrupted many a film. It has cost studios millions upon millions of dollars. It has teased fanboys looking for another sweet taste of their favorite franchise. And it keeps the rumor mill grinding away on hundreds of internet sites devoted to tracking and cataloguing the minute details of film production. It is where James Cameron was stuck in his attempt to make a *Spider Man* movie. Alan Moore's comic book masterpiece *Watchmen* has had a seat in DH for nearly 20 years alongside Indiana Jones (although, as of this writing, it looks like Drs. Jones and Manhattan may be pulled out of DH soon.)

I have a theory about Development Hell that I have shared with a few friends from time to time. I think movies are made when they are meant to be made. If it takes Peter Guber and Jon Peters over a decade to get the first *Batman* film made, then filmmaking fate meant for the project to wait for Tim Burton to come along. I feel the same about *Superman*. It really needed an unknown named Christopher Reeve to come out of nowhere and wow Richard Donner enough to get the lead role. Anyone out there think of Superman without thinking of Reeve anymore??? Anyone…didn't think so.

All of the truly great and even most of the truly good movies have some sort of fate, destiny, Hand of God, or whatever you want to call it playing a role in the production. The shark in *Jaws* keeps breaking down and forces Spielberg to be more creative…in fact, makes him show the shark less than planned and it actually is more effective. Tom Selleck is the first choice to play Indiana Jones, but can't get around his <u>Magnum, P.I.</u> schedule. So, the role goes to Harrison Ford. I could give dozens more examples of how fate interceded in a film's production, but you get the idea.

Movies are made when they are meant to be made. It's something I'd like you to keep in mind as you read the screenplay in your hands. We think the story behind the story is just as interesting as the script. This script started as a radio drama produced in Columbia, MO for a radio program I hosted and produced called "Theater of the Mind." The show ran weekly on community radio station KOPN 89.5 FM and it showcased radio theater from around the country. One of the mandates we had for the show was to create original, locally produced programming on a regular basis. We put together a great group of actors, writers, and directors for our initial batch of one hour shows and scheduled *Swindlers* as the first original show.

Due to the time constraints, my idea for the *Swindlers* story was to be pretty straight forward. I wanted something that could stretch the technical limitations we had as well as a story that had liberal doses of action and humor. As a lifelong sci-fi fan, I also decided I want to write something that would tweak the standard conventions of the genre especially more contemporary, popular fare like the two Stars: *Trek* and *Wars*. I wanted space ships on the frontier, robots, aliens, and a dashing, yet flawed hero to lead the way. And then, I wanted to turn it all upside down. *Trek* always focused on a crew saving the galaxy, following the rules, and serving the greater good. I wanted a captain and crew who were out for themselves. A group of flawed characters who would drive the story rather than respond to it. I wanted the anti-*Trek*.

Knowing what I wanted from the story, I cranked up some *Trek* soundtracks on the stereo and started banging out the script. I am definitely one of "those writers" who needs the appropriate accompaniment to write. Lots of James Horner and Jerry Goldsmith for the sci-fi stuff, John Carpenter for the horror stories, and a blend of classic rock and pop for the superhero comics. (I can't explain why I'm listening to the *Escape From New York* CD while writing this, but the President's plane is getting ready to crash and by the time I start the next paragraph, Snake will be arriving…)

The script for *Swindlers* is my personal record for fastest completion. Only a couple of weeks from idea to final draft(or as final as my drafts get. I'm very picky and always find something to tweak here and there. Guess I can't give George Lucas crap for the Wars Special Editions, huh?) I tend to do bits of rewrites on earlier portions of a script while still writing the first draft of the later sections. So, I don't know that I ever really do what you would call "rewriting." Until the deadline hits, I'm always changing phrasing or descriptions or plot points. It gets to the point that I need someone to pry it away from me. Luckily, with *Swindlers*, we had a recording session with the cast and once that was finished, it would be difficult to change things.

That's not to say the rewriting ended with the cast recording of the script. We still had to edit the music, sound effects, and dialogue together and make it fit into our one hour timeframe. Because of this, a big chunk of the palace scene with Bob, Vina, and Puraso was cut…removing some back story about Puraso's recently deceased wife. And the rewriting could keep coming until this puppy is made into a movie one day. Going over things for this publication of the script has given me some new ideas. Wow, I really need to let go at some point.

(For those of you who want to follow along with your *Escape From New York* soundtrack, the Crazies just attacked…try to keep up.)

When the idea of forming a company to create and produce genre entertainment in my hometown of St. Louis began to take root in my head, the first project I thought of was *Swindlers*. I dusted off the radio script and knew it wouldn't take much to reconfigure it into a film screenplay. The simple story was something I knew could be done for a lower budget, plenty of possible locations were in the area, and it's been awhile since someone had done a pretty straight-forward, family-oriented, original, action and adventure filled Sci-Fi Space Opera.

With my initial partner, Steve Newton, it was decided that we would move forward with *Swindlers* as our first attempt at a feature film project. Steve started on pre-production sketches and designs while I started splitting my time between finding funding and beginning the task of finding production staff.

Ask anyone who has tried to get a movie off of the ground. There is plenty of help and support for a project that doesn't really need it. Everyone will fall all over themselves to be a part of something that already has money and distribution in place. Find someone willing to take a chance on a new company with no money. If you can, will you give them this book and tell them to call us!!! Odds are you won't find anyone.

Oh, don't get me wrong. We found plenty of people who were nice and politely listened to our pitch before telling us to call them when we had investors. We had a representative for what she described as a "major" actor who was looking for independent projects to act in with his wife. I couldn't tell you who the actor is if you put a gun to my head. Not because I don't want to reveal them, I don't know who they are. The actor's rep would never reveal the supposed star's name. Ever!!! Not after exchanging numerous e-mails and phone calls. I've talked to potential investors who I would swear were involved in the mob. I've had friends of friends of friends who know someone who has lots of money fall through. I've talked to a number of people involved in media throughout St. Louis as well as tried to contact people who claim to be supporters of the Missouri film scene. I'm sure each and every one of them is very interested in this project. They just don't want to be the first people to jump into the pool.

The positive part of this process is the people who did jump into the deep end to join our attempts to get *Swindlers* made. They're all listed with heartfelt thanks in the acknowledgments. But, I want to point out Kelli Lerner in particular. Kelli made this journey through Development Hell worthwhile because she was one of the first "outsiders" to read the script and believe in the project.

There was a brief period where it appeared that we were close to landing local investors and had decided to move forward with casting. Kelli was great at making herself available to talk about actors and offers or even just what we were trying to accomplish with our company and my filmmaking philosophies. We had contacts with lots of name actors and came very close to getting a few of them to sign on before the investors dried up. I don't ever want to say that our first attempt to get this project off the ground was for nothing because I really learned a lot while we went through that process. And there are few feelings like watching Matthew Perry on the couch next to Jay Leno to hype his hosting of the ESPY awards and knowing that he is reading your script that very weekend. Kelli made that, as well as many other very cool moments like it, happen and one of these days, I'll be able to pay her back.

It was during those heady days of "Hey, so-and-so is considering our offer to play Jana and we're waiting to hear back from this actor about Bob" that the list of potential investors was coming to an end. We had run our pitch by people who knew the business and weren't in a position to help at the time…other people who thought they knew the business and really had no idea what they were doing…and a fair share of people who didn't know anything about filmmaking and would love to work with us in the future when their personal situations make it feasible. The problem was that we were starting to get actors to commit to the project and we needed to either move forward or pull the plug. I don't regret anything except the fact that we weren't able to get it going two years ago. But, sometimes the best thing to do is regroup and refocus. *Swindlers* wasn't going to be made into a movie in 2006, but Midnight Entertainment wasn't going to give up on our goals.

We wanted to be a company focused on character-driven, high-concept, genre entertainment produced locally in St. Louis, MO. And we weren't going to stop until that happened.

Now, as I'm writing this introduction, the calendar has turned to 2007 and we have a website featuring previews of our upcoming projects including *Swindlers*, an online store where you can purchase a wide array of Clock Tower and *Swindlers* logo merchandise, and we've even jumped into publishing with this book and other projects which are around the corner. We wanted to share this story of unsavory people becoming heroes and trying to save an alien planet in some way, shape, or form. We hope you enjoy it and spread the word about all of the pop culture-y goodness we have coming from Midnight. If we can get enough people interested, maybe Bob and the gang will find their way out of Development Hell sometime soon...

Jim Yetter

MARCH 2007

FADE IN:

EXT. THE WONDEROUS EXPANSE OF DEEP SPACE

Stars fill the black void. A multi-colored nebula can be seen in the distance. And a streaking comet passes by...

MCCAIN (V.O.)

Space...whoever said it was the final frontier should be shot out an airlock...without a spacesuit. Oh, it seems so full of adventure and excitement when you're a kid. But, let me tell you, it's not easy. Oh, sure, if you're an officer on one of those big Federation cruisers exploring the galaxy, it's great. Strange new worlds, discovering new life, blah, blah, blah. But, some of us have to work for a living. We have to worry about taxes and docking fees, and fuel costs...not to mention finding a crew that won't stab you in the back...bunch of freeloading pirates.

The camera pulls back to reveal that we have been looking through a portal and then pulls back more to reveal...

INT. MCCAIN'S CABIN

These are the quarters for entrepreneur/con man "Captain" Bob McCain. The cabin is small and not very tidy. McCain is seen sitting at a desk speaking into a handheld microphone.

MCCAIN

But, I digress. The book you are holding is a testament to the courage and fortitude of one great man who conquered the odds...rising from nothing to become...

The cabin's door buzzes and there is a knock from the outer corridor.

JANA

(From outside the door)

Bob? Hey, Bob, are you there?

MCCAIN

(Huffs) Recorder off.

JANA

(Teasing) Bob, you're not working on that memoir again, are you? You shut your comm panel off again. So, we figured...

MCCAIN

(Quickly stuffing the recorder in a drawer before going to the door)

What is it, Jana?

CUT TO:

INT. SHIP'S CORRIDOR

We see JANA KOREL, the ship's pilot, at the cabin door as it WOOSHES open revealing MCCAIN. JANA's blue hair and forehead ridges indicate she is clearly not human.

JANA

We picked up a planet with some rudimentary cities. Undeveloped culture, according to the computer. Mal and I think we should take a closer look.

MCCAIN

Did you do a mineral scan?

JANA

We're too far out for accurate readings, but we are picking up platinum and huge amounts of gold. It's everywhere. The computer's compiling the data...

We see her continue her report as they make their way to the bridge, but MCCAIN's v.o. fades in...

MCCAIN (V.O.)

You've heard of motley crews of pirates roaming the ancient seas? Well, motley doesn't even begin to describe my crew. (Fade Out)

JANA

And we registered an asteroid nearby. Mal thinks we should try the

JANA (cont.)

patented "McCain Manuever."

MCCAIN

You two have this all planned out, don't you? Getting to the point where you don't need me, huh? Thinking about going it alone, maybe?

JANA

You KNOW that only YOU have the control codes for the ship and the shuttle.

They reach elevator doors and enter the lift.

MCCAIN

As it should be. I'm not going to have history repeat itself and get left behind. What good is being the captain if your crew's just going to strand you one day?

JANA

When are you going to get over that? One time. We jumped into warp one time without you. We had to. The Feds were all over us and we had to leave. At least we came back for you.

The lift doors close as if on cue.

CUT TO:

INT. ELEVATOR

The focus is on JANA as MCCAIN describes his pilot.

MCCAIN (V.O.)

Jana Korel is the best pilot in the galaxy and if it wasn't for her shady past, she'd be flying one of the big Federation ships.

CUT TO:

INT. THE SHIP'S BRIDGE

The bridge has the worn look of a used military ship with an upper, horseshoe-shaped deck with several duty stations and a lower circular deck for the central command chair and a forward navigation console. There is a viewscreen mounted on the forward bulkhead currently showing a forward view. The elevator doors open onto the bridge. MCCAIN and JANA step out and move to their stations. To one side of the deck, the large wardroid TK-421 comes to life at their arrival.

TK-421

Captain Bob on the bridge. All hands at attention.

MCCAIN

At ease, big boy. At ease.

The robot lowers itself back into a less imposing position.

MCCAIN (V.O.)

TK-421 is an Achilles 9000 series Wardroid who was junked when
the new Armageddon series came off the assembly line. I saved him
from the scrap heap and now, TK's our muscle when things get
dicey.

MAL FECKS, the ship's engineer, pops up from an open access
space in the deck.

MAL

(Sarcastically) Well, well, well...look who decided to join us. (To
Jana) Convinced him to put the memoir on hold to take a look?

MCCAIN (V.O.)

Mal Fecks is my chief engineer. Okay, he's my only engineer. I don't
trust him as far as I could throw him, but he keeps everything
running. (Sparks begin shooting from the access hatch and MAL
jumps out of the hatch, banging the circuits with his tool.)
Well...almost everything.

MCCAIN turns to the engineer.

MCCAIN

Mal, do you know the 54th Iotian Precept? If not, look it up.

MAL

(Rubbing his chin) Hmmmm, Precept 54? Oh..."No matter where you go, there you are." Doesn't seem to fit...

JANA turns in her chair to join the fun.

JANA

(Jokingly) No, no, no. Precept 54 is "Never accept gifts from a three-armed Tholian."

MCCAIN

Alright, knock it off. If you people would read a book, you would know that Precept 54 is "Negativity destroys the mind."

A wireframe, holographic face appears floating in mid-air near the crew. This is the visual representation of the ship's central computer system.

COMPUTER

Actually, Precept 54 from the Iotian Book of Tulek is "The road to Oblivion is paved with good intentions." Perhaps, Captain, you are thinking of the Wanameh legend of Otamya who said, "Negativity is the ruin of all good men."

MCCAIN

(Growing more frustrated) No, I was thinking of the Iotian Precepts.
But, thank you so much for chiming in with your opinion.

COMPUTER

I live to serve.

MCCAIN (V.O.)

How could I forget to mention the ship's computer? As if she would
let us forget her. I imagine her programmer was a real "momma's
boy" who wanted to make dear old mom immortal by imprinting her
personality onto the ship. I hate him.

MCCAIN

Well, let's see this planet. Computer, bring it up on the screen.

The viewscreen changes to show the planet with overlays showing
various data such as population centers, natural resources, etc.

JANA

See...what did I tell you?

MCCAIN

Computer, overlay the mineral scan.

The screen changes again to show an overlay of mineral deposits covering the planet...platinum, silver, copper, and insane amounts of gold. MAL has moved from working on the access hatch to see the screen.

MAL

Look at it...all that gold. Just sitting there waiting for us to come and get it.

JANA

That's a million times more that we could spend in three lifetimes.

MCCAIN

Where's the asteroid? (Notices the blinking icon floating through space near the planet) Oh, I see it.

Near the planet is an icon showing the position of an asteroid with telemetry data appearing next to it. A dashed line shows the trajectory of the asteroid, which shows it gliding past the planet unharmed.

MAL (O.S.)

So, all we need to do is nudge it into a collision course with the planet.

JANA (O.S.)

Just like so.

The screen changes to show a new trajectory for the asteroid. This time it shows the rock impacting the planet.

JANA (O.S.)

We go down to the surface and show the inhabitants the imminent danger heading right for them.

MCCAIN

But, it just so happens we are in the business of removing threatening asteroids. Unfortunately, with times being what they are, it's an expensive proposition.

MAL

After all, there are fuel costs, disposal fees, taxes...

MCCAIN

But, we don't want to take advantage of these poor people in their time of despair. So, we will remove the asteroid without making a profit.

JANA

(Stepping up from her console) We will only need a small "fee" to cover expenses...

MAL

(Already dreaming of spending his share) The only problem is...

JANA

How much can we get out of them?

MAL

That's a pretty big rock. Do you think we can pull off changing its
trajectory?

JANA

(Turning to look at the screen) Sure, it's the same as any other rock
we've wrangled. (Starting to sound a bit unsure) Just bigger.

MCCAIN

(Standing from his chair) Look, we just slingshot around it, use its
own gravity to give us a boost of speed, snag it with the grappling
beams, and pull it along with us. Piece of cake.

MAL

(Not sounding convinced) Yeah, piece of cake. If the ship doesn't get
torn apart in the process.

Sparks fly from the open access hatch again.

MCCAIN

(Eyeing the hatch with concern) Something we should be worried
about?

MAL

Are we going to need the personal transporters for this?

MCCAIN

No.

MAL

Then, don't worry.

More sparks shoot out before Mal closes the hatch. Bob is still looking with concern at Mal and the hatch.

MAL

Relax...it'll be fine. (Turns to his station and mutters under his breath.) I hope.

MCCAIN

Alright, people, let's do this one by the numbers. Go to yellow alert.

TK-421, silent since being put "at ease" by Bob, comes to life again. An alarm sounds briefly and the bridge lights dim.

TK-421

Yellow alert, Captain Bob.

MCCAIN

Mal, keep me posted on how the grappling beams are holding up.

MAL

(Taking a seat at what is presumably the engineering station.) You've got it.

JANA

(Returning to the pilot's station) We are 10,000 kilometers from the asteroid.

MCCAIN

10,000 kilometers? Kilometers. Do you have to use metric? You know, some of us still like to use old-fashioned measurements...

COMPUTER

(As the wireframe face reappears) The UFP adopted metric standards for measurement in the year 2112. This standard was accepted in the Orion systems in the year...

MCCAIN

(Interrupting) That doesn't change the fact that I like feet, miles, and gallons! Now, go away!

The hologram disappears...

JANA

9,000 kilometers from the asteroid. Speed at one-half.

MCCAIN

(Looking annoyed at the kilometer reference) Make your speed one-quarter. Down angle 33 degrees. There you go...okay...level off.

COMPUTER (O.S.)

Collision alert. Collision with an object in one minute.

MCCAIN

We know. Don't worry. Jana can pull this off.

JANA

You hope.

MCCAIN

I haven't been wrong yet.

MAL

Unless you count that time at Orvela Three.

MCCAIN

Which I don't. That wasn't my fault.

JANA

7,000 kilometers...and I'm shutting down the engines.

MAL

Grappling beams standing by...

COMPUTER (O.S.)

Collision alert. Collision with an object in 30 seconds.

MCCAIN

Thank you sooooo much. Now, could you shut up?

COMPUTER (O.S.)

Fine, I do all of the heavy thinking around here and this is the thanks

I get. Well, when you are all dead, don't say I didn't warn you.

MCCAIN

We'll be dead. I don't think we'll be saying much of anything.

(Pause) I can't believe I'm arguing with a computer.

JANA

(Without taking her concentration off of the viewscreen or her

console) Could the two of you keep it down? I'm trying to slingshot

around an asteroid here.

MCCAIN

(Ignoring Jana) When I find the guy that programmed this ship...arrgghh...I'm going to kill him.

JANA

(Annoyed)Just as long as you do it after I keep us from smashing into this huge rock floating through space.

MCCAIN

Okay, okay...(Turning his attention back to their target) Get ready for thrusters. Four...three...two...one...now.

JANA

Full power!

CUT TO:

EXT. SPACE

The ship's engines roar to life as it approaches the spinning asteroid.

CUT TO:

INT. THE SHIP'S BRIDGE

The bridge begins to shudder from the strain of the engines at full power.

MCCAIN

(Over the roar of the engines) We're gaining speed.

JANA

We're only at 80 percent of our breakaway velocity!

MAL

She'll hold together.

The ship's hull starts to creak. MAL reaches out and rubs the console.

MAL

Come on, Baby. Hold together.

JANA

Velocity at 90 percent of breakaway...92 percent!

MCCAIN

Stand by on the grappling beams.

MAL

Yeah, I'm ready. (Under his breath as he looks at a display) You can do it, baby...just a little more.

A display on JANA's console shows the velocity percentage increasing...93...94 ...95…

The bridge shudders even more intensely.

                    JANA
                 96 percent.

                    MAL
    I hate to say "I'm giving it all she's got," but...

                   MCCAIN
                She'll make it.

                    JANA
              99 percent...100.

                   MCCAIN
             Hit the grappling beams.

CUT TO:

EXT. SPACE

As the ship's dual grappling beams shoot from the fore and aft of the lower hull, reaching to the huge asteroid. The ship is rocked by the opposing forces of its own irresistible force meeting this immense, almost immovable object.

CUT TO:

INT. THE SHIP'S BRIDGE

The bridge is rocked by the strain of grabbing the asteroid and the crew steadies itself by grabbing onto anything within reach.

JANA

Course correction locked in.

MCCAIN

Increase power to the shields.

TK-421

Shields have previously reached maximum output.

MAL

You better make this quick. We can't take much more of this.

Sparks fly from an unmanned station near TK-421. The wardroid reaches with one of its multiple armatures and extinguishes the fire with a blast of Carbon Dioxide.

JANA

Just one more second....and...we're there. Let it go.

MCCAIN

(To Mal) Grappling beams off. (Turning back to Jana) Move us
away from that thing.

CUT TO:

EXT. SPACE

The ship's grappling beams disengage and it quickly moves away
from the floating rock.

CUT TO:

INT. THE SHIP'S BRIDGE

More equipment blows up in a shower of sparks.

MAL

We've lost the forward shields and power to decks four and five.

MCCAIN

Computer, reroute power to compensate. (Looking to his crew) Is
everyone okay?

JANA

Other than my nerves?

TK-421

This unit is undamaged and fully operational.

MAL

Yeah, undamaged here too...for the most part.

MCCAIN

Okay...Jana, put us into orbit around the planet. Mal, take TK and
see what kind of damage we have. As soon as we know the ship's
condition, we'll go down and introduce ourselves.

DISSOLVE TO:

INT. SHIP'S ENGINEERING DECK

MAL FECKS and TK-421 are making their way down a corridor
stopping occasionally to inspect damage here or there.

MAL

(Mockingly) Mal, go check for damage. Mal, fix the engines. Mal,
we need warp speed in three seconds or we're all dead. (Pause) One
of these days they won't have Mal Fecks to order around anymore.

TK-421

It is imperative that you stay, Mal Fecks. TK-421 needs Mal Fecks
to repair this unit's systems when they malfunction.

MAL

See, even you think you can tell me what to do.

TK-421

TK-421 does not issue orders to Mal Fecks. Repair and Maintenance
is merely a need this unit has. The Achilles series is not self-
sustaining and requires support from qualified technical personnel.
You have proven to be more than qualified, Mal Fecks.

MAL

I guess that's as close as a machine can get to a compliment.

The pair comes to a door marked "Personnel Transporters", which
MAL proceeds to open. Smoke pours from the open doorway and he
waves it aside to survey the damage to the transporters.

MAL

Well, I guess we won't be transporting down to the planet.

He steps to a wall-mounted communication panel and punches a
button, bringing the panel to life.

MAL

(Speaking into the panel) Bob? Do you want the bad news first or the really bad news?

MCCAIN (O.S. FROM THE COMM PANEL)

It depends on your definition of bad.

MAL

Well, the teleporter's shot. We've blown the primary shield generator and the aft-firing laser battery if fried.

CUT TO:

INT. THE SHIP'S BRIDGE

MCCAIN is sitting in the command chair listening to MAL's report.

MCCAIN

What about the engines?

MAL (O.S. FROM THE COMM PANEL)

Well, it's going to take some time, but I should be able to repair them in time for us to leave. Give me a few days though.

MCCAIN

Make them a priority. We need the engines at full strength if we're going to move that rock again.

CUT TO:

INT. SHIP'S ENGINEERING DECK

MAL

Like I said, give me a few days. They're delicate. If I do a shoddy job, we could have a 500-megaton explosion on our hands.

MCCAIN (O.S. FROM THE COMM PANEL)

Do you have any good news?

MAL

We still have life support and the shuttle is intact, but the robot will have to pry open the shuttle bay doors so we can get to it.

TK-421

I am an Achilles 9000 series Wardroid, not a robot. A robot is a mindless automaton. This unit has the computing power equal to 5,000 Krellax supercomputers...

MAL

Okay, you're not a robot. For a machine, you're awfully sensitive.

CUT TO:

INT. THE SHIP'S BRIDGE

MCCAIN

(Rubbing his temples in frustration) Would you two stop fighting and get the shuttle bay doors open? We need to go down and meet our new friends.

DISSOLVE TO:

EXT. THE CAPITAL CITY OF GIRELLIA

Girellia is a world not yet industrialized, but rich in artistry and on the cusp of an age of discovery, a Renaissance World. The Royal Palace shows this richness of culture with colossal statues flanking the drawbridge entrance and colorful banners showing the Royal crest.

VINA (O.S.)

Father, I know you have a cabinet meeting soon, but I've come to ask for just a few minutes of your time.

PURASO (O.S.)

Vina, I always have time for my only child.

VINA (O.S.)

It's not time for me...I've brought Ruafo...

CUT TO:

INT. OF THE ROYAL CONFERENCE ROOM

PURASO and his ADVISORS are preparing for a meeting. They surround a large circular table with various scrolls and books on it. Along one wall is a crude slate writing board with facts and figures on it to be used during the cabinet meeting. VINA is standing near her father. The ADVISORS look annoyed at the mention of RUAFO's name. PURASO looks angry.

PURASO

RUAFO! How many times must I waste time with his baseless theories about the cosmos?

VINA

(Trying to calm him) I know, father. Ruafo has made minor miscalculations in the past...

ADVISOR #1

As well as outlandish, reckless pursuit of his idea that there are other civilizations...living on other worlds.

The Cabinet advisors chuckle at this until they notice PURASO is not laughing.

VINA

Perhaps, it is jealousy that causes our advisors to dismiss Ruafo's ideas.

ADVISOR #1

Jealousy? Preposterous!

VINA

He WAS correct about the migration of Vermicious Knids to our northern farmlands and that it would cause numerous crop losses. But, did anyone bother to listen?

PURASO

Daughter, need I remind you, that it is your childhood friendship to Ruafo that keeps me from ending his Royal sponsorship altogether.

VINA

My friendship with him has nothing to do with my belief in some of his theories. Please, Father...this time I believe he has information you should at least look at.

PURASO

Alright, Vina. But, if it is incredulous...this will be the end of
Ruafo's sponsorship from the Royal Treasury.

VINA goes to the entrance and motions for RUAFO. The scientist
enters carrying various books and charts rather clumsily before
spilling his evidence on the conference table.

RUAFO

Supreme Puraso, leader of our people...

PURASO

I know who I am, Ruafo...get on with it.

RUAFO

Oh, sorry...(To the gathered advisors) Ministers...

The ADVISORS grumble in acknowledgement before taking their
seats.

RUAFO

Right...well...I am humble in my miscalculations of the past.
Although, as I'm sure the Science Minister will agree, there has been
a theory or two that I was proven correct on.

ADVISOR #1

A few dozen Knids running over a hill to eat doesn't make you a genius...

PURASO

Gentlemen, I have a busy schedule and will not waste it on petty bickering. So, Ruafo...have we detected signs of life on the third planet again? Or are the Ice Caps going to melt and flood the continent?

RUAFO

Well, sire, I have brought something very interesting.(He shuffles through various charts, finds copies of the one he needs, and begins to hand it to the nearest advisor) Here you are...just...um...pass them around. There are copies for everyone.

The advisor pass copies around the table, like children in school, until the final one ends up with Puraso.

RUAFO

We have developed a way of creating pictographs from the observatory's telescopes. You can see in the first pictograph a large planetoid which we have been following for the past few days.

ADVISOR #1

Sire, this planetoid is no danger to us. I calculated its path myself a

few days ago. Its course takes it past our planet without

consequence.

RUAFO

As we thought until this morning.

PURASO

What happened this morning?

RUAFO

(Finding another set of pictographs and distributing them) Well, as

you can see from these new images, the object remains on course

until this second, smaller object enters the frame.

The pictograph shows a fuzzy image of the asteroid with our heroes

ship, small and barely recognizable, coming into the frame.

VINA

And the planetoid mysteriously alters its path.

PURASO

Vina...please.

VINA

But, Father, there is something in the frame.

RUAFO

I believe this smaller object may be a vessel of some kind.

PURASO

An alien craft?

ADVISOR #1

It's too fuzzy...

ADVISOR #2

We can't even make out what this other object is.

PURASO

Could it be a natural phenomenon?

RUAFO

Our technology for producing these images is very new and we are

still trying to analyze...

PURASO

Do you have proof it is an alien craft or not?

RUAFO

(Dejected) We have no proof...yet.

PURASO

Then, you will turn over your findings to the Science Ministry...

BATRAM, Puraso's aide, enters the room in a hurry.

RUAFO

I was hoping to continue investigating...

VINA

Father...

PURASO

The people of Girellia need facts...not groundless speculation.

BATRAM

Master...

PURASO

(Ignoring his aide) I have given you and your friend latitude in the

past because of your friendship.

BATRAM

(Trying to get Puraso's attention) Master, I...um...

PURASO

(Still ignoring him and getting angrier at Vina and Ruafo) Now, unless strange visitors from another planet come down here and announce themselves, I will not listen to any more nonsense.

BATRAM

MASTER!!!

PURASO

(Turning to him) WHAT!!!

BATRAM

There is a situation developing at the edge of the city.

PURASO

What kind of situation?

BATRAM

There are visitors who wish an audience with you.

PURASO

Have them schedule an appointment!

BATRAM

They say that they come from...the Cosmos.

PURASO

(Instantly turning from anger to gratitude as he addresses Ruafo and Vina) Perhaps I was too harsh on you. Let us see what these visitors have to say.

DISSOLVE TO:

EXT. OPEN FIELD NEAR THE EDGE OF THE CITY

The crew's shuttle sits in the middle of the field surrounded on all sides by a large, and growing larger, crowd of Girellian on-lookers. Most of the crowd is staying at a cautious distance, but a group of younger people have moved in for a closer look.

VARIOUS ON-LOOKERS

Look at the size of that...Is it a transport?...What is that?...Would you look at them?...That thing must be some sort of weapon...It looks scary...Watch out!...The monster's moving...

MCCAIN, MAL, and JANA are near the shuttle waiting for some authority to arrive. TK-421 moves to protect them from the crowd.

TK-421

Attention, citizens of Girellia, disperse immediately...

MCCAIN

(Stepping between the machine and the scared crowd) Whoa, TK, calm down. They're just curious.

Mal notices a group of youths getting a little too close to the shuttle's engines.

MAL

Hey, don't touch that! You'll end up breaking it! (To MCCAIN) You better hope someone shows up to handle this crowd, Bob. Curiousity killed the cat and we're next on the menu.

MCCAIN

Don't worry. Just take it easy.

TK-421

Attention. Military units approaching. 25 life forms from the south, southeast.

MCCAIN

(Under his breath) It's about time. (To the crew) You know the drill. Everyone remember your lines this time. And, TK, try to stay calm.

MCCAIN (cont.)

We don't need you shooting the place up like on Malmori, okay?

TK-421

TK-421 will not act until ordered or the ship's crew is in imminent

danger.

JANA

(Trying to reassure TK) These people don't look too hostile.

The Girellians part to make way for PURASO's party.

BATRAM

Visitors, the people of Girellia welcome you. All hail the great

Puraso.

PURASO, followed by a small group of guards, the advisors, Vina,
and Ruafo, enters the field and approaches the shuttle before
stopping at a safe distance.

PURASO

As the leader of my people, I welcome you. These are my advisors.
(He waves a hand toward them.) And my daughter Vina.

Vina gestures to remind him about Ruafo.

PURASO

Oh, yes, and Ruafo, one of our scientists.

VINA

Ruafo is responsible for discovering your...uh...ship.

PURASO

(Glaring at her before turning his attention back to the crew) Yes, among other discoveries. Well, we are curious about how you have come to our world.

RUAFO

(To PURASO) And don't forget about what they were doing around that planetoid...

MCCAIN

I am Captain Bob McCain and this is my crew. (Gestures to the others) We travel the galaxy searching for asteroids that can be mined of their resources. We found an interesting specimen and were preparing to file a report when we noticed that it was on a collision course with your planet...

The crowd stirs at this revelation.

PURASO

Citizens, please...let the visitor finish.

MCCAIN

As I was explaining, we are just a survey team. Usually, they send a

bigger mining ship after us to do the heavy work. (Starting to get

into playing the part) That takes months for the paperwork and

processing. (Very melodramatic) I hate to say it, but I don't know if

there is any way to save your planet.

JANA begins using a handheld scanner.

VINA

This is terrible. There must be something we can do.

Still acting as if she is consulting the scanner, JANA is ready to take

part in the ruse.

JANA

(To herself before looking up) And cue the miraculous solution. (To

MCCAIN, sounding optimistic) Captain, I've been taking some

readings. You should take a look at this.

MCCAIN

(To the Girellians) Excuse me for a moment. (Turning and huddling

around the scanner with Jana) Jana, just keep nodding as if I'm

giving orders.

JANA

(Quietly) Think they're going to buy it?

Meanwhile, PURASO's group is also having a secretive discussion.

RUAFO

(Pulling PURASO aside) This would explain the other object in my pictographs.

ADVISOR #1

But, something of that size couldn't just change its course without some sort of force acting on it.

PURASO

What are you saying?

VINA

(Very mistrusting) What if they moved it on purpose?

PURASO

Preposterous! Why would they move it on purpose?

VINA

One thing is certain. It is very convenient that they showed up out of nowhere.

RUAFO

We must watch these visitors closely.

PURASO

Speak no more. They return.

MCCAIN approaches the group. We can see his crew near the shuttle in the background.

MCCAIN

I apologize, Great Puraso. My pilot was giving me an update on the asteroid. It may be possible for us to help you.

PURASO

Really?

VINA

How interesting...

MCCAIN

Well, it won't be easy. Our engineer will need to make some upgrades to our ship. And we will be using a great deal of our fuel reserves.

MAL

(Calling from the shuttle) Did you tell them about the upgrades?

MCCAIN

(Turning towards Mal and holding a hand up to silence him)
Yeah...just getting to it. (Mockingly rolling his eyes as he turns back
to PURASO) Sorry about that. But, he is right. This is going to cost
us quite a bit. If only we had found some gold on that asteroid...

PURASO

Gold, did you say? Why we have this metal in excess on Girellia...

VINA

(Interrupting to stall for time) But, Father, it would take some time to
gather an adequate supply.

ADVISOR #1

Perhaps, the visitors could use this time to...um...uh...upgrade their
ship, did you say?

MCCAIN

Yes, I did. We'll need a few days to prepare our ship.

RUAFO

(Following Vina's lead) And we could use this time as well...to
analyze our data and formulate a plan of attack.

PURASO

(Jumping in as well) Exactly! Ruafo, while the Science Ministry

PURASO (cont.)

examines OUR data, perhaps you could work with one of the

Captain's crew to analyze THEIR findings.

MCCAIN

(Unsure of how to proceed) Okay...Let me discuss my orders with

the crew. We may be able to assist with gathering the gold more

quickly. And my pilot can assist your scientists.

VINA

(With false appreciation) We will gladly accept any help you and

your crew can give, Captain.

MCCAIN

Please, call me Bob.

VINA

Bob, then.

MCCAIN

Well, I guess I'll have my people get in touch with your people and

we'll get to work saving your planet.

PURASO

(Breaking into MCCAIN and VINA's moment) Very well, Captain.

The people of Girellia thank you. I look forward to our next meeting.

MCCAIN

As do I. (Nodding to him) Great Puraso. (Taking VINA's hand and kissing it) Milady Vina. (To the others) Don't worry. We'll do our best. (Turns to the shuttle and begins barking orders as he approaches) Okay, people, let's get to work. Jana, you're going to be working with the scientists. (Fades into the distance) Mal, you get back to the ship and start the upgrades...

VINA

Were you planning on offering them a guided tour of our mines? What were you thinking, Father?

PURASO

Gold is plentiful and I would give it all to save our world.

VINA

We don't even know who they are or if they can help. We must be careful with these visitors. Something just doesn't feel right.

RUAFO

I will find out what I can from the pilot, but someone should stay close to this "Bob" person.

PURASO

Leave that to Vina and me. We will offer him our hospitality (Calling out to MCCAIN) Captain, perhaps if you have the time, we

PURASO (cont.)

can interest you in a tour of our Royal Palace. To pass the time while we transfer the gold to your ship.

At the shuttle, MCCAIN turns to answer.

MCCAIN

Hmm. (Calling back) That would give us an opportunity to discuss our plans. Give me a few more minutes with my crew. (Turns back to the crew) Anyway, Jana, you've got to find out what these scientists know. They seem really twitchy, especially the younger guy. He knows more than he's letting on. Mal, set up TK with the cargo transporter near the mine. Get the goods rolling up to the ship and then head back to start the repairs. You can leave TK in charge of the gold transfer.

TK-421

TK-421 endeavors to serve, Captain Bob.

MCCAIN

Great, big guy. So, any questions?

JANA

(Looking towards PURASO's group) They're looking pretty antsy over there. Think they trust us?

MAL

If you were them, would you trust us?

JANA

Good point.

MCCAIN

Hey, everything's going to plan so far. Let's keep our heads together.
(To MAL) You get the ship ready to leave in a few days. (To JANA)
And you, find out how much they know. Okay, let's go.
The crew meets the Girellian group in the middle of the field.

PURASO

Is everything in order?

MCCAIN

Yes. My engineer and droid are going to start helping your miners
with the gold transfer. And my pilot is ready to begin briefing your
scientists.

PURASO

Very well. (Gesturing to the scientist) Ruafo, will take Miss...

JANA

(Introducing herself) Jana...Jana Korel.

PURASO

Yes...Miss Korel, if you will follow Ruafo, he will take you to our
Ministry of Science.

RUAFO

(Sarcastically) I'm sure we have much to learn from your more
developed knowledge.

PURASO

My chief of staff, Batram, will take care of the gold arrangements.
That just leaves you and I, oh...and Vina, to discuss our plans. This
way, Captain.

MCCAIN

After you...

As the various parties go their separate ways...

VINA

Captain, tell me, how is it that you can speak our language without
ever having been here?

MCCAIN

Well, we have this device. (Fumbling for it) Here it is...a translator.
Let me show you how it works...

DISSOLVE TO:

EXT. THE FIELD LATER IN THE DAY

Most of the crowd has dispersed, but a few curiousity seekers still remain. A child of about 8 or 9 years old is climbing onto one of the rear engines.

MAL

(Exiting the shuttle and seeing the child) Hey, kid...get off of there before you get hurt.

Mal pulls the child off of the engine as two older, pre-teen girls come running up to them.

DANI

Watto, Niba and I have been looking all over for you! Mother is furious!

WATTO

I was just looking at the cool ship.

MAL

Looking at it? You've been using it for a jungle gym!

The children look puzzled at his reference.

NIBA

(Nervously) Dani, we'd better go before your mother and my parents

send out a search party for US.

DANI

You're right. (Ordering sternly) Come on, Watto.

WATTO

But, I wanted to see more of the...

Suddenly, TK-421 enters the girls view directly behind WATTO.

DANI AND NIBA

(SCREAM)

From TK's view, the small boy slowly takes in the robot's huge

frame with widening eyes...

WATTO

Cool...

TK waves an armature to disperse the children.

TK-421

Make way, small creatures. You must maintain a minimum distance

TK-421 (cont.)

of 5 meters from this unit for safety.

NIBA

Dani, that...that thing...

DANI

I know...it talks...and it's really, really big.

TK-421

The Achilles 9000 is 4 meters high and is mounted on impact-resistant adamantium tank treads capable of travel over any terrain.

MAL

They don't want to hear a sales pitch, you dumb machine. You kids better run along. (Turns to head back into the shuttle.)

WATTO

(Looking over all of the machine's attachments) Hey, check out all of this cool stuff...

TK-421

You are referring to the twin 500 kilowatt Melboranz lasers (the weapons slide into action on each of his main arms) and 50 millimeter shoulder-mounted pulse cannon. (The cannon flips into ready mode on his right shoulder.)

WATTO

(Unsure of what TK is saying) Umm...I guess so.

TK-421

The Achilles 9000 is also equipped with a chest mounted M-P-S guided rocket launcher and a vibranium-alloy armor. (A panel in his chest opens to reveal a very nasty-looking rocket launcher.)

NIBA

This thing's a monster. We'd better get out of here.

DANI

(Even more demanding) Watto, let's go...

WATTO

I'm talking, Dani. You're not the boss of me. (To the robot) So, what's your name?

TK-421

I am designated unit TK-421, formerly of Starhawk platoon Gamma.

WATTO

I'm Watto.

DANI grabs WATTO by the arm.

DANI

You're going to be dead when Mom gets a hold of you. Now, let's

go.

WATTO

(Struggling) Hey, let go of me! DANI!!!

Seeing the conflict between the children, TK's weapons systems

come online.

TK-421

Hostile actions observed. Weapons systems activated.

MAL

(Running in from behind him) Hey...wait a minute, you

knuckleheaded droid!!!

Mal gets between the kids and the robot.

TK-421

They are engaging in hostile actions. This unit's programming calls

for ending all hostile actions with minimal casualties.

MAL

(To the children) Go on home, kids. (Turns back to TK) They're just

brother and sister. Kids do that. I should know. Spent most of my

MAL (cont.)

formative years being tortured by three older sisters myself.

TK-421

Mal Fecks was tortured?

MAL

It's a figure of speech. (Shakes his head) Why am I trying to explain this to you? You're a ro...I mean, automaton. You'll never understand relationships.

From across the field, WATTO stops to wave at his new friend.

WATTO

Bye, TK-421...I'll see you later.

MAL (O.S.)

See, he's laughing now. They're just kids.

TK-421

Kids...they are small creatures.

MAL

Yeah, small creatures without a care in the world. They don't even realize that there's a huge chunk of space rock that could wipe them off the face of this planet.

DISSOLVE TO:

EXT. GIRELLIAN MINISTRY OF SCIENCE HEADQUARTERS

RUAFO and JANA exit the building and walk down a path.

JANA

I hope I was of some help in explaining your data and pictographs. I just wish we could figure out what caused the asteroid to change course like that.

RUAFO

(Suspiciously) Yes, I'm sure you do. (Changing the subject) So, Miss Korel, not only are you a scientist in your own right, but you also pilot your ship?

JANA

Among other things...we're a small crew. So, we double up on the assorted duties and jobs around the ship. My primary duty is as pilot.

RUAFO

And science is one of your many specialties?

JANA

It is now. We've been short a science officer for about a year now. I'm the only one with any background in science...such as it is.

RUAFO

Don't take offense, but you don't have ANY formal science background?

JANA

Other than some basic courses at the Academy before I dropped out? Not really. I am interested in the mysteries out there, though. Strange phenomena, exciting encounters with new life...kind of like this.

RUAFO

(Dropping his hostility a bit) I envy you, in a way. Every day, you travel to places I have only dreamed of.

JANA stops and looks at him.

JANA

I was like that too...until I got out there. Trust me. Not everybody flying through space has grand adventures. It's not like we're a Federation cruiser with nothing to do but glorified high school science projects. Those of us in the private sector have to work for a living.

RUAFO

But, couldn't you still make time to explore the wonders around you and discover? You are actually OUT THERE...in the cosmos. If it were me, I wouldn't let those opportunities pass me by.

JANA

Don't you think I want to be out there hopping galaxies and having adventures? Some of us have to be more practical, more responsible.

RUAFO

I would think that out there, in the Cosmos, adventure would be all around you. Perhaps, you just have to be looking for it.

RUAFO turns and continues walking down the path, leaving JANA behind.

JANA

(Mockingly) Perhaps, you just have to be looking for it. (Pause) I've been looking. Where's the adventure?

RUAFO stops, realizing JANA is not following. He turns to her from further down the path.

RUAFO

Are you coming?

JANA

Yes...sorry...lead on.

DISSOLVE TO:

INT. PRIVATE AUDIENCE CHAMBER OF THE ROYAL
PALACE

An ornate throne sits on a raised dais. Various tapestries, paintings,
sculptures, recovered artifacts, etc. are on display around the room.
PURASO and VINA are giving MCCAIN the grand tour.

                              MCCAIN
(Examining the various decorations) Great Puraso, you have a
            wonderful palace here. Who's you're decorator?

                              PURASO
Many of these sculptures were recovered from the Lost City of
            Bilagio Natte...authentic Fifth Dynasty.

                              MCCAIN
            (Feigning interest) Ah...the lost city, you say?

They gather around one particular sculpture.

                              PURASO
Yes. You see, the Fifth Dynasty was ruled by Galen the Second...

                               VINA
Father, the captain doesn't have time for a history lesson.

MCCAIN

No, it's all veerrryyyy interesting. But, please, call me Bob. I've

never liked titles.

VINA

I apologize...Bob. But, enough with small talk and history.

PURASO

(Shocked at her candor) Vina, the captain is our guest.

VINA

(Ignoring that MCCAIN is even in the room) And he is also the man

who claimed to be able to help us. I just thought it would be nice for

him to explain how he's going to do that.

During this exchange, MCCAIN can be seen between father and

daughter trying to be nonchalant.

PURASO

(Similarly ignoring MCCAIN's presence) The man said they were

professionals...

VINA

He has said a lot of things...

PURASO

What choice do we have but to give him the benefit of the doubt?

VINA

Well, we could ask him if he has a plan other than to take a ship full
of our gold and run...

MCCAIN

Wait just a minute...

PURASO

Captain, please...this does not concern you...

VINA

Yes it does. We're arguing about him!

PURASO

Oh...right.

VINA

(To MCCAIN) Well, do you have a plan?

MCCAIN

Oh, is it my turn now? Well, of course we have a plan.

MCCAIN looks around for some props to demonstrate his plan. He finds his props in the form of a sphere-shaped sculpture...

PURASO

(Worried about him damaging the sculpture) Captain, please...that
piece is priceless.

MCCAIN

Don't worry. (Turning his attention back to looking for one more
item. He spies one of VINA's jeweled brooches.) Excuse me,
milady.

VINA

(Taken aback) Captain, really...

MCCAIN holds the sculpture, representing the asteroid, and the
hairpin, representing his ship. During his explanation, he moves the
two objects to demonstrate the maneuver.

MCCAIN

Okay, so we'll use our ship (Indicating the brooch) and travel around
the asteroid (Indicating the sculpture), using the asteroid's own
gravity to gain more speed...

VINA

Is this maneuver a common one to perform?

VINA and PURASO continue watching the demonstration. PURASO is very concerned about the safety of the priceless sculpture throughout.

MCCAIN

Sure...in fact, back in the old days, they used to call this the "Coyote Thrust Maneuver." Anyway, after we gain enough speed to break away, we grab the asteroid with our grappling beams and pull it along with us. We should be moving at a sufficient velocity to move it just enough that it will pass by your planet.

PURASO immediately takes the sculpture back and places it on the near-by pedestal. MCCAIN returns the brooch to VINA who fastens it to her blouse properly again.

PURASO

The preliminary reports we have received from the Science Ministry have eased our apprehension a bit. Based on their projections, the asteroid should land in the middle of our largest ocean. Ruafo even predicted that due to the object's relatively small size, it should cause nothing more than minor tidal disruptions along the coastline.

MCCAIN

(Sensing a problem) Supreme Puraso, I don't mean to cast doubt on their assumptions. I mean, I'm sure they're all fine people. But, our computer has calculated more accurate projections.

PURASO

As you've said...I just don't understand how the Ministry can be that far off in their analysis.

MCCAIN

When you're dealing with physics and spacial mechanics of this scale, even a minor error can be costly. It's best to let the computer handle the calculations.

VINA

(With an edge of sarcasm) We must seem very backwards to you, Captain. Your high technology must be too far beyond our meager comprehension.

MCCAIN

I apologize...I didn't mean to offend...

PURASO puts a reassuring hand on MCCAIN's shoulder, maneuvering him to a table with refreshments.

PURASO

(Pouring the group drinks) Ruafo and my daughter have been life-long friends, Captain. At times, she allows her loyalty to get in the way of logic...

VINA

Father!!!

PURASO

It's true, Vina. (To MCCAIN, while handing him a goblet) If you
will excuse me, Captain. I must find Batram for an update on our
progress.

MCCAIN

Of course.

PURASO leaves the room. MCCAIN and VINA are left with an air
of tension. He starts to make a comment at which she turns to
examine a tapestry.

MCCAIN

You know, I can usually read people fairly well. I've got the feeling
you don't like me very much.

VINA

Oh, you are very charming and handsome. Everyone is falling all
over themselves to help you save our planet.

MCCAIN

I feel a "but" coming...

VINA

But, everything just seems too perfect. The asteroid just happens to change course mysteriously. You just happen to be in the area. Somehow the Ministry of Science's smartest minds are wrong and your computer just happens to be right. When things are too perfect, something usually goes wrong.

MCCAIN

How could someone as optimistic and open as your father have a daughter...

VINA

(Interrupting) So cold and pessimistic? Well, Captain. When I was younger, my mother became very sick. None of us knew because she kept it a secret. Every day, she would wake up and make the whole day perfect for my father and me. When she died...when we found out the truth, I knew those days weren't perfect. I knew they had all been lies to protect me from reality.

MCCAIN

I'm so sorry.

VINA

I don't need you to be sorry. Just know that for my father, there are no grey areas. All of his decisions are very simple. Either right or wrong. "If there is an asteroid threatening us and someone says they

VINA (cont.)

can help, well then, let them save the day." That's how he thinks.

But, I see the grey areas. I know things are never what they seem.

MCCAIN

Don't worry. I don't plan on disappointing him.

VINA

No one ever plans for bad things to happen, Captain McCain. They

just do.

DISSOLVE TO:

INT. THE SHIP'S BRIDGE

The elevator doors open and MAL walks out humming to himself.

As soon as he steps onto the bridge, the computer's holographic face

appears.

COMPUTER

It's about time someone came back. I was beginning to wonder if the

natives had made a feast of you or sacrificed you to one of their

quaint, little gods or some other nonsense. (Disappointed at the

realization that MAL is alone) Oh, it's just you, Mal.

MAL

What is that supposed to mean?

COMPUTER

Nothing. Are you by yourself?

MAL

Yes. You know, I wish you would give me a little more respect than
that. I'm the one who keeps you running after all.

COMPUTER

(Sarcastically) If I had a body, I'd bow down to your supreme
magnificence. But, I don't...so, you're out of luck. Now, what's going
on down there?

MAL

(As he gets to work at the engineering console) Well, the robot's
working on transferring the gold and Bob and Jana are running
interference with the locals.

COMPUTER

If I wanted the short version, I'd ask TK-421. You're
human...embellish it a little. Give me the juicy details.

MAL

(Sighs) Okay...there's a boy who thinks TK is his new toy, Jana's

MAL (cont.)

fighting with one of the scientists, and Bob's laying it on pretty thick for the ruler's daughter...Mina or Tina...something like that. Anyway, you know Bob...

COMPUTER

Yes. And so do half the women in the galaxy, single or not. Why, do you remember that time on Philestis III...

MAL stands suddenly, not wanting to get stuck in a long conversation with the lonely computer.

MAL

(Rushing to the elevator platform) Sorry. I'd love to stay and chat. But, I've got less than 48 hours to get the ship up and running. Got to go.

The elevator lowers MAL away.

COMPUTER

Sure...just run along. I'll be fine. I'll find something to do. I know. I'll calculate Pi to the 483rd decimal place again. That'll only take two or three nanoseconds. See...done already.

DISSOLVE TO:

EXT. GIRELLIAN GOLD MINE

Various miners and other workers are scurrying around, trying to get the gold transferred to the ship in record time.

VARIOUS MINERS

Alright, bring up the next load...that's 25 down, 10 more to go...We've only got 10 more hours...come on, let's get moving...

BATRAM, PURASO's Chief of Staff, is near the cargo transporter platform checking over a report with the mine's FOREMAN as TK-421 approaches.

TK-421

Is there any assistance I may give?

The FOREMAN leaves to supervise the miners.

BATRAM

(Turning towards the robot) I think they have things in hand. Just be ready to operate this transporter device of yours. The next load is coming soon.

TK-421

Very well. TK-421 will await further instructions.

WATTO can be seen dodging workers as he makes his way to the robot.

                              WATTO
                    Hey, TK-421...it's me.

The child is out of breath as he reaches TK. The robot turns to him.

                              TK-421
        Watto, it is very late. This is not a secure area for small creatures.
        You must return to your place of residence immediately.

                              WATTO
        (Catching his breath) But...they said...they said you were leaving in
        the morning and I wanted to say goodbye. And I wanted to give you
                                this...

WATTO holds out a makeshift looking necklace made of leather and
a rock. He hands the token of affection to the robot. TK uses one of
his manipulator arms to take it.

                              WATTO
        See...(Revealing a similar necklace around his own neck) I've got
                    one too. So, we don't forget that we're friends.

TK-421

This unit can never forget. TK-421 has 597 septillion terabytes of memory storage. Now, return at once to your place of residence.

The robot begins to turn back to the work at hand and WATTO reaches up to stop him.

WATTO

Wait...will you come back and visit?

TK-421

Why would this unit need to return to Girellia?

WATTO

Cuz we're friends and you're supposed to want to be with your friends. If I could visit you on your ship, I would. But, my parents wouldn't let me.

TK-421

This unit does not understand.

DANI comes into view and sees her brother with the robot.

DANI

Watto...

She runs between them.

DANI

What are you doing all the way out here? It's the middle of the night!

WATTO

I'm just saying bye to TK-421, that's all.

DANI starts to grab WATTO, then looks to TK...remembering his reaction from earlier. Cautiously, she turns back to WATTO.

DANI

You're lucky that mom and dad are still asleep. Come on, before you get us both in trouble...again.

WATTO

But, he isn't coming back! He doesn't understand about being friends and stuff. I tried to tell him that he's my friend...

DANI

And it'll never understand. Niba's uncle said it was just a machine...they called it a robot or something.

TK-421 rises up at this statement.

TK-421

TK-421 is not a robot. A robot is a mindless auto...

DANI

(Interrupting) Whatever you are, you're a machine. Not a person. And not something that can be a friend. (To WATTO) It doesn't understand.

WATTO

(Confused) But, he's trying to help us and that's what friends do.

DANI

It's helping us because that Captain guy told it to. It's just following orders like a soldier. Now, come on.

The children turn to leave, but WATTO turns back to the robot. The child reaches out to the machine.

WATTO

I don't care what she says, TK-421. You're still my friend and I hope you come back to see us. Goodbye...

TK-421

Goodbye does not compute with this unit.

DANI (O.S.)

See...I told ya so.

WATTO

(Turns to his sister) Shut up, Dani.

The children run into the distance. TK watches them leave and we slowly focus on one of his armatures until WATTO's token of affection slips into view, dangling from the robot's hand.

DISSOLVE TO:

EXT. AN OPEN FIELD NEAR THE EDGE OF THE CITY

The crew's shuttle comes in for a landing causing the gathered crowd to shy away at first. After the dust settles, the crowd gets a bit closer. The entrance ramp lowers, revealing MAL. MCCAIN, JANA, and TK-421 approach.

MAL

So, who's ready to blow this popsicle stand?

JANA

(Sarcastically) It's the tactful side of you that I love, Mal.

MAL

(Clueless) What did I say?

JANA rolls her eyes.

MCCAIN

Could you two attempt to be civil for the next few minutes? We're almost out of here. (Turning to the robot) TK, get that cargo transporter loaded.

TK-421

Right away, Captain Bob.

MCCAIN

See, the big guy knows how to behave.

MAL

The "big guy" is nothing but ten billion micro-circuits and a ton of tritanium alloy. We could teach him to roll over and play dead if we wanted.

MCCAIN

Ha, Ha, Ha...very funny. Now, look sharp. Puraso and the others are coming to see us off.

JANA

(Worried) You're not going to want to make a big speech, are you? (MCCAIN begins to walk toward the approaching group, ignoring her) Bob? Hey, remember what happened last time?

MCCAIN, without turning back to the crew, waves her off

nonchalantly. The crowd parts for PURASO's party and they enter the field.

RUAFO

But, Supreme Puraso, I don't know how the calculations could be this far off from...(venomously)...these people. Your own ministers verified my initial analysis. This asteroid will not hit land.

PURASO

That's enough of this discussion. We have made an agreement with the Captain and I will not jeopardize the lives of our people.

VINA

I just don't know if we can trust...(Seeing MCCAIN approaching, she quickly changes to a sunnier tone)...Captain McCain, there you are.

MCCAIN joins the Girellians before they reach the shuttle.

MCCAIN

Excuse me, if I'm interrupting...

VINA

No, no...everything is fine. Why?

MCCAIN

(Confused) Why?

VINA

(Stumbling) Why? Why...Why we were just discussing...

PURASO

(Stepping in) Discussing the...um...well...

VINA

Evacuation plans. If you're pilot's information is correct, we should
be prepared to evacuate.

RUAFO

In the event that you're mission should fail.

MCCAIN is taken aback by this. He feigns wounded feelings.

MCCAIN

Puraso, you must have confidence in my crew. We've done this
maneuver a doz...(reaching for more hyperbole)...a hundr...thousands
of times. Never fear.

VINA

Just the same, we will continue with our preparations.

RUAFO

And we will continue analyzing our data. Just in case we missed
something important.

MCCAIN

Sure. You can never be too prepared. Why the people of Iotia have a

saying...Precept 78, if I recall...

MAL and JANA are waiting impatiently at the shuttle's entrance
ramp.

MAL

What's he doing, now? If he's getting ready to make a speech...

JANA

(Yelling to MCCAIN) Uh, Captain...we really should be going.

Back in PURASO's group, MCCAIN is annoyed at JANA's
interruption.

MCCAIN

(Holding a finger up to JANA) Just one more minute...(Back to

Puraso) I apologize, Great Puraso. Now, where was I? Oh, yes,

Precept 78.

JANA (O.S.)

Bob, remember the big chunk of space debris hurtling towards this

planet?

MCCAIN

(Closing his eyes to calm his frustration) I'm aware, thanks. (Opens his eyes and returns to his charming persona) Anyway, the Iotians are great philosophers. I'll have to bring you a copy of the Precepts the next time we're in the area.

PURASO

(Extending his hand to MCCAIN) Good luck, Captain.

MCCAIN

And to you. (To Vina) Good luck to you all.

PURASO

Girellia will hope for your success.

VINA

And prepare for your failure.

MCCAIN

That's certainly an encouraging note to leave on.

MAL and JANA enter the shuttle with MCCAIN following up the ramp. MCCAIN pauses at the top of the ramp. The engines come to life as MCCAIN turns back to the crowd.

MCCAIN

(Raising his hand to the crowd) People of Girellia...Live long and...

Suddenly, he is cut off as MAL's hand grabs him and pulls him into the shuttle. The ramp closes as the shuttle lifts off. Most of the crowd is shouting and waving to the crew as the shuttle blasts into space.

DISSOLVE TO:

EXT. SPACE

The ship floats majestically through space as the asteroid travels along its path in the background.

CUT TO:

INT. THE SHIP'S BRIDGE

The elevator rises into view, carrying MCCAIN, JANA, and MAL. TK-421 can be seen rising from an access hatch near his station.

MCCAIN

Okay, let's move this asteroid back and get to spending that gold.

JANA

Sounds great to me.

She steps down and takes her place at the navigation console. Then, the COMPUTER's holographic face appears.

COMPUTER

Hello, nice to see everyone made it back.

MAL

(Oblivious to the COMPUTER) I think I'll see things through down in the engine room. I had to patch things up pretty quick and I don't want the engines to fall apart.

COMPUTER

Okay, that's fine...ignore the computer who keeps your ship running and life support online.

MCCAIN

(Also ignoring the COMPUTER) Keep us posted on our status, Mal.

MAL

Will do.

MCCAIN

(Finally seeing the COMPUTER) Hey, computer, do you have the calculations done on moving the asteroid yet?

COMPUTER

Oh, now you want to chat? Never mind MY feelings...MY
needs...just "Hey, computer, keep the shields up" or "Computer, help
us from falling into a black hole." It's never "Computer, how was
your day?"

MCCAIN

Will you give us the results, pretty please?

COMPUTER

Very well. To keep the asteroid from hitting the planet Girellia, you
will need to move it three degrees on its y-axis and four-point-six
degrees on its z-axis.

MCCAIN

That's not too bad.

JANA

(Entering a new course into her console) This is still going to be
tricky since the ship's not up to par.

MCCAIN takes his seat in the command chair.

MCCAIN

True, but when has it ever been up to par? (Touching the
communication control) Mal, are you ready?

MAL (O.S. FROM THE COMM PANEL)

The mains are bypassed like a Christmas tree. So, don't give me too many bumps.

MCCAIN

No promises. Bridge out. (Switches off the comm) Okay...Jana, bring us up to fifty percent power and move us in.

CUT TO:

EXT. SPACE

The ship's engines power up and it glides towards the asteroid.

CUT TO:

INT. THE SHIP'S BRIDGE

JANA's hands move flawlessly over her console, guiding the ship into its new course.

JANA

Seven thousand kilometers and closing.

MCCAIN

Let's make this just like last time...without all of the damage to the

MCCAIN (cont.)

ship. Oh, and Computer, if I hear one word about a "Collision Alert"...

COMPUTER

Fine. If you want to smash headfirst into an asteroid, see if I care.

JANA

Please don't start arguing again. This was tough enough the first time. Ten seconds...nine...eight...

CUT TO:

INT. SHIP'S ENGINEERING DECK

MAL moves from panel to panel, keeping an eye on things.

JANA (O.S. FROM THE COMM PANEL)
Seven...six...

CUT TO:

INT. THE SHIP'S BRIDGE

MCCAIN starts clutching the armrests of the command chair nervously.

JANA (O.S.)

Five...four...three

MCCAIN

Computer, stand by with the grappling beams...

JANA

Two...one. Full power.

The engines roar to life and the bridge starts to vibrate slightly.

MCCAIN

Grappling beams on!

CUT TO:

EXT. SPACE-NEAR THE ASTEROID

The ship's grappling beams engage the asteroid as before. This time the stress on the asteroid causes a spray of rock and debris to smash into the ship.

CUT TO:

INT. THE SHIP'S BRIDGE

The ship is rocked with the impact of the debris. The crew does their best to hold on.

JANA

We're getting hit with some debris from the asteroid.

MCCAIN

Hold her steady.

MAL (O.S. FROM THE COMM PANEL)

Bob, we're losing power to decks three and four. I'm rerouting power to the grappling beams, but we can't hold on much longer.

An unmanned panel erupts in sparks and the deck starts shaking more violently.

MCCAIN

Hang on...we're almost there.

A few more sparks shoot from various systems.

TK-421

Shields weakening. Down to thirty percent.

JANA is trying her best to hold on to the console while still flying the ship.

JANA

Give me thirty more seconds.

CUT TO:

INT. SHIP'S ENGINEERING DECK

Several panels ignite in a shower of sparks and flame.

MAL

We've lost the shields and power to the forward grappling beam.
We've got to shut down or we're gonna blow.

CUT TO:

INT. THE SHIP'S BRIDGE

JANA can feel the ship straining and their time running short.

JANA

Bob...I need more time. Bob...

MCCAIN senses that they have not succeeded and may lose the ship
and their lives if they don't stop.

MCCAIN

Damn...shut us down. Computer, deactivate the grappling beams.

JANA

Mal, are you alright down there?

MAL (O.S. FROM THE COMM PANEL)

I'm a little overcooked, but I'll be fine.

MCCAIN

Computer, check the asteroid's new course.

JANA

I hoped we moved it enough.

COMPUTER

Based on our readings, the asteroid will impact still impact Girellia.

MCCAIN

Damn...

JANA

Computer, where will it land?

COMPUTER

The asteroid will impact 180 degrees, 42 minutes, and 30 seconds by

COMPUTER (cont.)

60 degrees, 28 minutes, and 20 seconds.

MCCAIN

In English?

JANA

Computer, overlay those coordinates onto a map of Girellia. (Her
eyes grow wide as she looks at the screen) Oh, no...

MCCAIN

(Standing and looking from the COMPUTER to JANA) Does
somebody want to clue me in?

The viewscreen shows a globe-like representation of Girellia with
various oceans and continents. One of the continents has an orange
area hi-lighted. The asteroid is shown moving towards the planet and
a dashed line from the asteroid to the orange area shows its
trajectory.

JANA

That orange area that the asteroid will impact...that's the Girellian's
capital city. We didn't move the asteroid out of their way...

MCCAIN

We moved it into a direct collision course...

DISSOLVE TO:

INT. THE SHIP'S BRIDGE-AN HOUR LATER

MAL is sitting at his station fiddling with one of his tools while JANA paces back and forth on the lower deck. TK-421 sits quietly in his corner.

MAL

(Breaking the silence) So, we weren't able to move it out of the way. We knew this might happen sooner or later.

JANA

(Interrupting) That makes it all better.

MAL

Hey, it's not exactly our fault that the ship isn't in the best shape. Let's just notify the Feds and let them move it. We can high tail it before they get here.

JANA

(Sarcastically) That's a great idea! Oh, wait...no, the closest Fed ship is three days away.

TK-421

(Coming to life) The asteroid will impact Girellia in two days. The

TK-421 (cont.)

Federation ship will not reach this system in time.

MAL

(To TK) You stay out of this. (Back to Jana) And you, I'm just

saying...

JANA

You're just saying we should take the money and run.

MAL

Well...yeah...

TK-421

This unit is programmed with a number of prime directives.

Directive Delta: "All Achilles units will act to preserve the life of

neutral parties and will not allow through the unit's actions or

inactions for that life to be harmed." Watto is a small creature and a

neutral party. TK-421 cannot allow Watto to be harmed.

JANA

That's what I'm talking about. These people were counting on us and

we messed up.

MAL

So, if we go back, how are we going to save them? Besides, when did you start caring about responsibility?

JANA

Maybe I've just realized that the Feds don't have a monopoly on
doing the right thing and helping people.

TK-421

TK-421 will return to Girellia and defend Watto. This unit will need
your assistance, Mal Fecks.

MAL

You are both crazy!

They are interrupted by the elevator rising into view. MCCAIN steps
onto the bridge oblivious to the others.

MAL

Hey, Bob...

JANA

Bob? Are you okay?

MCCAIN

(Lost in his own thoughts) Hmm...oh, Jana...Mal...

TK-421 stirs to life again.

TK-421

Captain Bob, this unit requests reassignment to the planet Girellia. TK-421 must defend the small creature designated Watto from the approaching asteroid.

JANA

TK, give him a minute. (Pause) Uh, Bob...we've been talking and...

MAL

And these guys are nuts. There is nothing we can do to fix things. The ship is damaged too much to move that asteroid again.

MCCAIN

I've been in my cabin thinking...we spend so much time looking for the next planet we can scam that we never stop to think about the people we leave behind. We get so wrapped up in playing the game that we never consider the consequences for anyone other than ourselves. And for what? Gold. Well, it's not going to buy us absolution from this.

MAL

Well, I'm glad everyone's feeling sorry for themselves and the Girellians. But, that doesn't change the fact that there is nothing we can do about it.

MCCAIN

Maybe not. But, we need to do what we can. The only real difference between us and those people on the Federation ships is the decisions we make. I think it's time to make the right choice for once. I'm going back.

JANA

(Stepping forward) Me, too.

TK-421 moves forward.

TK-421

It is an operational imperative that this unit protects Watto.

MAL

That's just great...you know we don't have a snowball's chance...

MCCAIN

You don't have to come, Mal. We'll give you the shuttle and enough supplies to reach the nearest starbase.

MAL

(Considering his options slowly) Of course I don't HAVE to go. But, the guilt will eat at me while I get the shuttle ready. By the time I'm ready to go, you would have found my soft spot and convinced me to

MAL (cont.)

stay. We might as well bypass all of that and get to work.

JANA

(Hugging MAL) I knew you couldn't leave.

MAL

Sure you did. Anyway, if I filled the shuttle with supplies, there
wouldn't be any room for the gold. I'd be alive, but penniless. At
least this way, I can die a rich man.

MCCAIN

(Rubbing his hands together) Okay, let's get to work. We have to
find a way to save this planet.

DISSOLVE TO:

INT. THE SHIP'S BRIDGE-TIME PASSES

The crew looks as if they have been brainstorming for hours.
MCCAIN is spinning around aimlessly in the command chair. MAL
is slumped over his console and JANA is back to pacing the lower
deck.

MCCAIN

So, after all of this brainstorming, we have...

JANA

Absolutely nothing.

MAL

I don't know. I kinda liked the robot's idea.

TK-421

This unit is not a robot...

MAL

(Blowing him off) Yeah, yeah, yeah...

MCCAIN

Hey! Let's not forget that we're on a timetable here.

JANA

I just don't see how we can move the asteroid anymore without

tearing the ship apart or blowing it up in the process.

MCCAIN

Computer, I've noticed you've been quiet. What's your analysis?

The Hologram appears.

COMPUTER

My analysis concurs with Jana.

MCCAIN

That's it? There's nothing we can do.

COMPUTER

As much as it pains me to do so, I would have to agree with Mr. Fecks. The best course of action would be to send a distress signal to the nearest Federation ship. They will be better equipped to deal with the disaster relief.

MAL

(Lifting his head slightly) See, I told ya so...

JANA

(Angrily) MAL!!!

TK-421

The nearest Federation starship is 3.2 days away at maximum speed. That ship would arrive too late to protect the Girellians. Watto must survive.

JANA

(Collapsing into her chair) So, we're back to square one. Rip the ship apart or have it blow up on us.

MCCAIN

(Standing and taking Jana's place pacing the deck) Rip the ship up or

MCCAIN (cont.)

have it blow up. (His mind starts working and you can almost see the gears moving as he thinks) Rip it up or...blow it up. That's it! We'll blow it up.

JANA and MAL are stunned.

JANA

What???

MAL

That's crazy!

MCCAIN

What will the destructive yield be if we overload the ship's engines and blow it up?

MAL

500 megatons...but, Bob, come on...blow the ship up???

MCCAIN

(Starting to fall in love with his plan) Sure, we overload the engines and escape in the shuttle. We'll be stranded on Girellia, but it could move the asteroid enough. Couldn't it? Computer, do the math.

COMPUTER

I did the calculations two nanoseconds after the words left your mouth. Such an explosion would move the asteroid enough for it to miss the planet by a hair, cosmically speaking.

MCCAIN

There you go. (Barely containing himself) I love this plan. I'm glad to be a part of it.

JANA

Wait...how do we set the ship to explode AND give ourselves enough time to get clear?

MCCAIN

The computer can blow the engines for us while we escape.

COMPUTER

I really hate to burst your bubble, but I am programmed for self-preservation. I can't act in any way to damage myself or the ship, including something suicidal like this.

JANA

Then, someone will have to stay behind to hit the switch...

TK-421

To ensure the survival of this crew and the people of Girellia, this

TK-421 (cont.)

unit will volunteer to initiate the ship's destruction.

COMPUTER

I thought we machines were supposed to stick together.

MAL

Yeah, good idea, TK should do it.

JANA

Why...because he's a robot...(To TK) Sorry, automaton...(Back to
MAL) Just because he's artificial, he should automatically stay
behind. Why shouldn't it be someone with the technical know-how
to do it?

MAL

In that case, you've got just as much know-how to blow up the ship...

MCCAIN

(Stepping in between) Guys...if anyone's going to stay behind, it will
be me.

JANA and MAL immediately stop arguing at this statement and
looked at MCCAIN with surprise.

MCCAIN

I'm the captain and I got us into this mess. You'll need TK to keep

you out of trouble. And TK needs Mal to keep him running.

(Turning to JANA) And Mal needs you to keep him honest.

JANA

But, Bob...

MCCAIN

No, if we wait, I'll think of some way out of this and the Girellians

are running out of time. Trust me. I'm not doing this because I

WANT to die. But, someone has to and I'm responsible. Now, take

TK and get the shuttle loaded with supplies. (To MAL) Mal, you'll

wire everything into the navigation console for me.

The others just stand motionless. The realization has hit them and

suddenly, they don't want to leave.

MCCAIN

(Smiling and trying to lighten the mood) Come on, this isn't like it's

the first time you've abandoned me to my fate...

JANA

(Defending herself) The Feds were all over...

MCCAIN

I know, I know. Just joking. Now, get going to the shuttle. And Mal, get to work on that destruct sequence.

MAL and JANA enter the elevator, leaving MCCAIN alone on the bridge. After they have left, he takes a moment to reflect before sitting in the command chair.

MCCAIN

Well, Bob, this is certainly a fine mess you've gotten yourself into.

DISSOLVE TO:

INT. THE SHUTTLE BAY

The crew is gathered in front of the shuttle one last time before they leave.

MAL

Now, you remember the sequence? It's blue, red, green...then, code in three-alpha-six.

MCCAIN

Why do destruct sequences have to be so complicated? Just give me a button to push...one button, that's all I need.

MAL

Don't screw around. Blue, red...

MCCAIN

(Reassuring) I've got it, I've got it. Now, all of you get out of here.

TK-421

TK-421 directive Alpha states "This unit must place the safety and continued survival of Captain Bob McCain above all other directives."

MCCAIN

I know. I made that your Prime Directive when I got you. Now, you have a new one. Protect Mal, Jana, and your new friends on Girellia. I'll be fine.

MAL and TK-421 start for the shuttle, leaving JANA behind to say good-bye. She is fighting back tears, not wanting to get emotional.

JANA

So...this is it.

MCCAIN

Hey, don't get misty on me. You're supposed to be the tough one, remember.

JANA

I've been trying to think of something to say...

MCCAIN

I know. Whatever you're thinking...I already know.

JANA

I've been thinking that I've been missing out on

something...adventure, discovery, excitement. Everything that

happens on other ships to other people...

MAL

(From the shuttle's entrance ramp) Jana, let's go. We're burning

daylight.

JANA

(Wiping a tear away) It's just... It's been right in front of me the

whole time. I just took it for granted. This is the adventure I've been

searching for.

MCCAIN

(Hugging her, trying to stay positive) So, hold on to that. Now, get

going...Take care of those two. They'll need it.

JANA turns and runs up the ramp as it starts to close. The shuttle's

engines ignite and large Bay door opens. MCCAIN watches as the shuttle lifts off the deck before launching into space.

MCCAIN

(Smacking himself on the forehead) I forgot to tell them to have the
Girellians build a big statue of me. Oh, well...

DISSOLVE TO:

INT. THE SHIP'S BRIDGE

The elevator rises and deposits MCCAIN onto the upper deck. He
starts to make his way to JANA's navigation console.

MCCAIN

(To himself) Let's see. It was...red, green, blue...(Stops) No,
no...Green, red, blue...Damn, oh, wait...

The computer's Hologram appears near him.

COMPUTER

The correct sequence is blue, red, green...then, code in three-alpha-
six.

MCCAIN

I thought you couldn't commit suicide?

COMPUTER

I can't, but can I help it if I remember everything you people say?

MCCAIN sits at the console and begins entering the sequence.

MCCAIN

Okay...blue, red, green...three...alpha...six.

The bridge's lighting changes to a red hue and an alarm sounds. A slowly building hum also can be heard through the bulkhead.

COMPUTER

Engine overload. Critical mass in three minutes.

MCCAIN

Computer, overlay the course of the shuttle on the viewscreen and give me their current distance.

The information appears on the viewscreen showing the shuttle moving away from them slowly.

COMPUTER

The shuttle's current distance is 2,000 kilometers.

MCCAIN

And what's the minimum safe distance?

COMPUTER

With the shuttle's shields at full power, it will survive the blast at

6,000 kilometers.

MCCAIN

Keep giving me updates.

COMPUTER

Engine overload in two minutes thirty seconds. Shuttle distance at

2,500 kilometers.

MCCAIN

Come on, get your speed up.

COMPUTER

Wait, the shuttle is reversing course. 2,400 kilometers and closing.

MCCAIN

What the hell are they doing, coming back?

CUT TO:

INT. THE SHUTTLE

JANA is sitting in the pilot's seat while TK-421 and MAL are in the

aft compartment. MAL is scurrying around with various tools and electronic components, while TK is rummaging through several containers.

JANA

(Over her shoulder, not wanting to take her eyes off of the controls)

Hurry up, you two! We'll be within range soon. We've only got a minute to pull this off before I have to put all of our power back into the engines to get us out of here.

MAL

We're going as fast as we can! Rewiring a cargo transporter to accept a human pattern isn't easy, you know!

TK-421

This unit demands your immediate attention and all possible haste, Mal Fecks! We must save Captain Bob!

MAL

(Carrying his load next to the robot) I'm trying, you stupid tin can! Now, hand me that spanner.

CUT TO:

INT. THE SHIP'S BRIDGE

MCCAIN is looking at a transmission from JANA on the

viewscreen.

MCCAIN

You're doing what?!?

JANA

(On the viewscreen) We're going to use the cargo transporter to get you off the ship before it explodes.

MCCAIN

(Condescending) But, the cargo transporter can't accept complex patterns. Thus, the fact that they are only used for CARGO and not PEOPLE.

JANA

(On the viewscreen) We know. Mal's working on that.

From behind JANA, electrical sparks fly and MAL can be heard howling in pain.

MCCAIN

What was that?

JANA

(On the viewscreen, Trying to cover-up) Nothing.

MCCAIN

It didn't sound like nothing. Jana, I appreciate the gesture, but stop.
Don't risk yourselves on this crazy rescue.

JANA

(On the viewscreen) Don't worry about us. It's our choice.

MCCAIN

Well, then, I'm worried about me. Have you seen what happens
when a human goes through a cargo transporter? It's not a pretty
picture.

JANA

(On the viewscreen) You'll just have to trust us. Our ETA is thirty
seconds. So, get ready.

The transmission ends and is replaced on the viewscreen by an
image of the shuttle drawing closer.

MCCAIN

Great. I went from being blown to kingdom come to having my
molecules rearranged in the wrong order. If I weren't such a
pessimist, I'd think things were looking up.

The computer's Hologram appears.

COMPUTER

At least this way, you have increased your chance of survival by a

factor of five.

MCCAIN

But, the odds of me surviving were a trillion to one before.

COMPUTER

See...now, they are only 250 billion to one. Cheer up, Bob.

CUT TO:

INT. THE SHUTTLE

MAL is busy working on the cargo transporter while JANA is flying
by the seat of her pants.

JANA

(Glancing quickly over her shoulder) How's it going back there?

We're getting close.

MAL

I know. Just a few more seconds. (To TK-421) Hey, Mister
"Computing power of 5,000 Krellax Supercomputers," get over here.

The robot rolls over to the transporter unit.

TK-421

How may this unit assist you, Mal Fecks?

MAL

I need to run the transporter through your processor so that Bob
doesn't get scrambled like an egg.

TK-421

This unit does not understand the connection between Captain Bob
and the early life stage of a chicken.

MAL

I'll explain later. Now, open up your access port.

A panel on the robot's side slides open revealing various jacks and
circuits. MAL attaches a cable from the transporter to TK-421.

MAL

Now, I'll plug you in here and...voila, cargo transporter changed into
a personnel transporter in record time. Mal, you are a genius.

From the forward section, JANA turns in frustration.

JANA

Hey, genius, quit your yapping and fire that thing up already.

CUT TO:

INT. THE SHIP'S BRIDGE

MCCAIN is fidgeting nervously at the navigation console.

COMPUTER

Engine overload in one minute thirty seconds.

MCCAIN

I think now would be a good time to rescue me.

COMPUTER

Engine overload in one minute twenty seconds.

MCCAIN

Yeah, now would definitely be a good time.

JANA appears on the viewscreen.

MCCAIN

Jana?

JANA

(On the viewscreen) We're ready over here. Mal says it's going to take a few seconds to lock onto you. So, be patient.

MCCAIN

At this point, what choice do I have?

COMPUTER

Engine overload in one minute.

MCCAIN

Thanks, computer. Let's go, Jana. (A light bulb goes off in his head)

Hey, Jana, download the computer's core memory to the shuttle.

Might as well save her too.

COMPUTER

Engine overload in forty seconds.

JANA

(On the viewscreen) We won't get it all transferred in time.

MCCAIN

Just do it.

COMPUTER

Thank you, captain. Engine overload in thirty seconds.

JANA

(On the viewscreen) Hold still, transporter is locked.

A shimmering field of energy begins to surround MCCAIN and he slowly disappears into nothingness.

CUT TO:

INT. THE SHUTTLE

Everyone is stationed as before: JANA piloting the ship, TK-421 plugged into the transporter, and MAL monitoring the equipment.

> JANA
>
> Did we get him?

> TK-421
>
> Processors are sorting the pattern and beginning reintegration sequence.

> MAL
>
> You better hope your processors are up to the challenge. I don't know if I want to watch.

The cargo transporter comes to life with a shimmering field of energy. Slowly, a twisting, writhing figure begins to take shape. The reintegration is taking a long time to sort and put back together MCCAIN. The shuttle's interior lights dim several times and a maintenance hatch blows open in a shower of sparks and debris.

MCCAIN

(Slowly, while still being reintegrated) Do...you...think...you...(Now, fully integrated) ...could have cut it a little closer?

MAL

Yes!!!

JANA

You made it!!!

TK-421

This unit is pleased for your survival, Captain Bob.

MCCAIN steps down from the transporter platform and pats the robot's shoulder turret.

MCCAIN

So am I. (Looking at MAL) You shouldn't have come back.

MAL

Jana made us. She said...

JANA

(From the pilot's station) I just said that we wouldn't be much of a crew without a captain. Plus, we were getting a bad reputation for deserting and leaving our captain behind to die.

MCCAIN

(Approaching JANA in the forward compartment) Thanks...I mean
it.

COMPUTER (O.S.)

Excuse me...anyone there?

MCCAIN

(Surprised, trying to find the source of the voice) Computer? You
made it.

COMPUTER (O.S.)

Not all of me, but most of the good parts. I still have my sparkling
personality.

MAL

(Joining them) Wonderful.

COMPUTER

Although, I seem to be missing parts of my memory. I know I was
doing something before you sucked me into the shuttle...just can't
remember...

MCCAIN

The countdown!

JANA

(Returning her focus back to the controls) Hold on!

The shuttle lurches as JANA reverses their course.

MAL

How much time's left?

MCCAIN

Couldn't be more than thirty seconds? Computer...how much time is

left?

COMPUTER (O.S.)

Oh, I don't know...twenty...nineteen...four... fifty-seven...eleven...did

I say four?

MCCAIN

Thanks for the help. (To JANA) Punch it, Jana.

CUT TO:

EXT. SPACE

The shuttle rockets away towards Girellia. In the background, the
approaching asteroid and MCCAIN's ship can be seen.

CUT TO:

INT. THE SHUTTLE

Tension mounts as the crew watches and wait. A readout on the viewscreen shows their distance from the soon-to-explode ship.

                              MAL
              5,000 kilometers...we're not going to make it.

                            MCCAIN
                         We'll make it...

The readout continues to climb reaching 5100...5200...5300...5400...and so on.

                             JANA
                        How long before...

CUT TO:

EXT. SPACE

The shuttle has widened the distance just as the ship explodes in a huge fireball with multi-colored waves of energy cascading outward from the blast. The force of the blast hits the asteroid causing it to erupt in smaller disruptions of rock and gasses. The shuttle, meanwhile, is caught trying to outrun the waves of energy and force rippling from the explosion. It is rocked by the forces.

CUT TO:

INT. THE SHUTTLE

The cabin is being shaken by the concussive waves. MCCAIN and MAL are slammed around the forward compartment. JANA is trying to maintain control of the shuttle while holding onto the console for stability. Shortly, the rocking and shaking subsides. The crew regains their footing. TK-421 enters the forward compartment from the rear to help MAL to his feet.

MAL
(To TK) Thanks.

TK-421
It is an operational imperative of this unit to help friends.

MAL smiles at this.

MCCAIN
Everyone in one piece.

JANA

I think so. The shuttle's still holding together.

MAL

(Patting a bulkhead) She'll make it to Girellia.

COMPUTER (O.S.)

In case, anyone is wondering, I'm fine. Although, wasn't our ship a
lot bigger than this?

MCCAIN

(Smiling) You know…things haven't always worked out for us, but
I've got a new outlook on life. I think we've got a bright future ahead
of us.

JANA

There's a whole galaxy out there to explore.

MAL

And lots more treasure to find.

TK-421

There are many more defenseless people to protect.

MCCAIN

I think the Iotians have a precept that covers this...

JANA

Oh, no...

MAL

Here we go again...

CUT TO:

EXT. SPACE

As the shuttle drifts towards the planet Girellia, with the Girellian
sun setting behind the planet.

MCCAIN (O.S.)

I think it's number seventy-five...or maybe number thirty-four...

FADE TO BLACK

THEN...A TITLE CARD ZOOMS INTO VIEW SHOWING...

"THE SWINDLERS WILL RETURN IN..."

AND THE CAPTION IS OBLITERATED BY THE FORCE OF A
LOGO BLASTING THROUGH...A LOGO FOR...

"THE DECEIVERS OF FATE"

Afterword:

The Continuing Voyage Through Development Hell (2014)

What a long, strange trip it's been. 15 years of Bob and Jana…The Girellians and TK-421…Mal and a starship's computer that takes nagging to a championship level.

I still cross paths with the original Swindlers crew from time to time, those amazingly creative actors who brought my characters to life, and it makes me smile to remember our rehearsals and recording sessions for the initial radio version of this story. As I type this, we are in the process of producing a brand new version of Swindlers featuring all new music, sound effects, and a full cast of actors bringing these characters to life once more.

Unfortunately, we lost the great Willy Wilson who played Puraso in the original cast. Willy was a great actor and even better gentleman…someone I had the honor and pleasure of knowing for nearly 20 years when he passed away. Luckily, we live in the digital age and I still have the DAT tape master recordings from 15 years ago. When a new version of Swindlers started to become a reality, I spoke with Willy's wife Vicky to get her blessing to include Willy's performance as Puraso in the new version. She happily agreed and, using the magic of digital editing, Willy will portray the ruler of

Girellia once again along with a new vocal cast in the remake. It is my hope that we can entice a few other original cast members to join us as well.

And that is only the beginning. This anniversary edition has several extras in the Bonus Material section. However, the most secret and special surprise is on the last page of the script itself. This is the first place ever that I have shared the name for a sequel story. The Deceivers of Fate is actually one of two possible titles I've had in my head since Swindlers premiered in 1999. And I have shared them with no one…until now.

One of the reasons we decided to create a new version of Swindlers was to find a cast that could carry us through other stories. There will be a trilogy at least. Swindlers in 2015, Deceivers in early 2016, and the third in late 2016.

I owe much to these characters and this story. Writing it started me down a long, twisting path that has led to other creative doors opening, personal and professional relationships starting that continue to this day, and, most importantly, it was the first project from a fledgling small press publisher with a clock tower logo.

The development hell I find myself in now is much different than that which I was stuck in 7 years ago. Now, it is a hell of my own creation and I control the direction of the journey. It is a journey that has us creating more stories for you and finding other kindred spirits to join our crusade. In the coming year, we have several new projects coming your way involving superheroes, time travel stories, and a possible horror project in time for Halloween.

When I began writing Swindlers in 1999, I never imagined it would have a life beyond its radio broadcast or a small release on CD. Now, digital downloads, e-books, and podcasts are a thing! The pathways to get content released have multiplied exponentially in the new millennium. And Midnight is taking advantage of them.

The previous 15 years have taken us across the country to spread the word about Swindlers. From Los Angeles to Nashville and several stops in-between. We have met great people who are enthusiastic about reading great Sci-Fi and Fantasy. I can't wait to see where the next 15 years takes us and how many more fellow fans we meet.

Thank you for joining us on this trip. We are telling these stories because we have a need to entertain you with thrilling adventures and exciting characters. I hope you enjoy what we have to offer and come back for more. Trust me, we have lots to share with you…

Jim Gellert

December 2014

BONUS

MATERIAL

Since you've read a screenplay, it's only right that we include our own version of DVD extras!

The following pages include pre-production sketches and storyboards for the unproduced film version, as well as a list of all of the various sci-fi and fantasy easter eggs included throughout the script.

First up, let's take a look at the opening pages from an aborted graphic novel adaptation with artwork from Steve Newton…

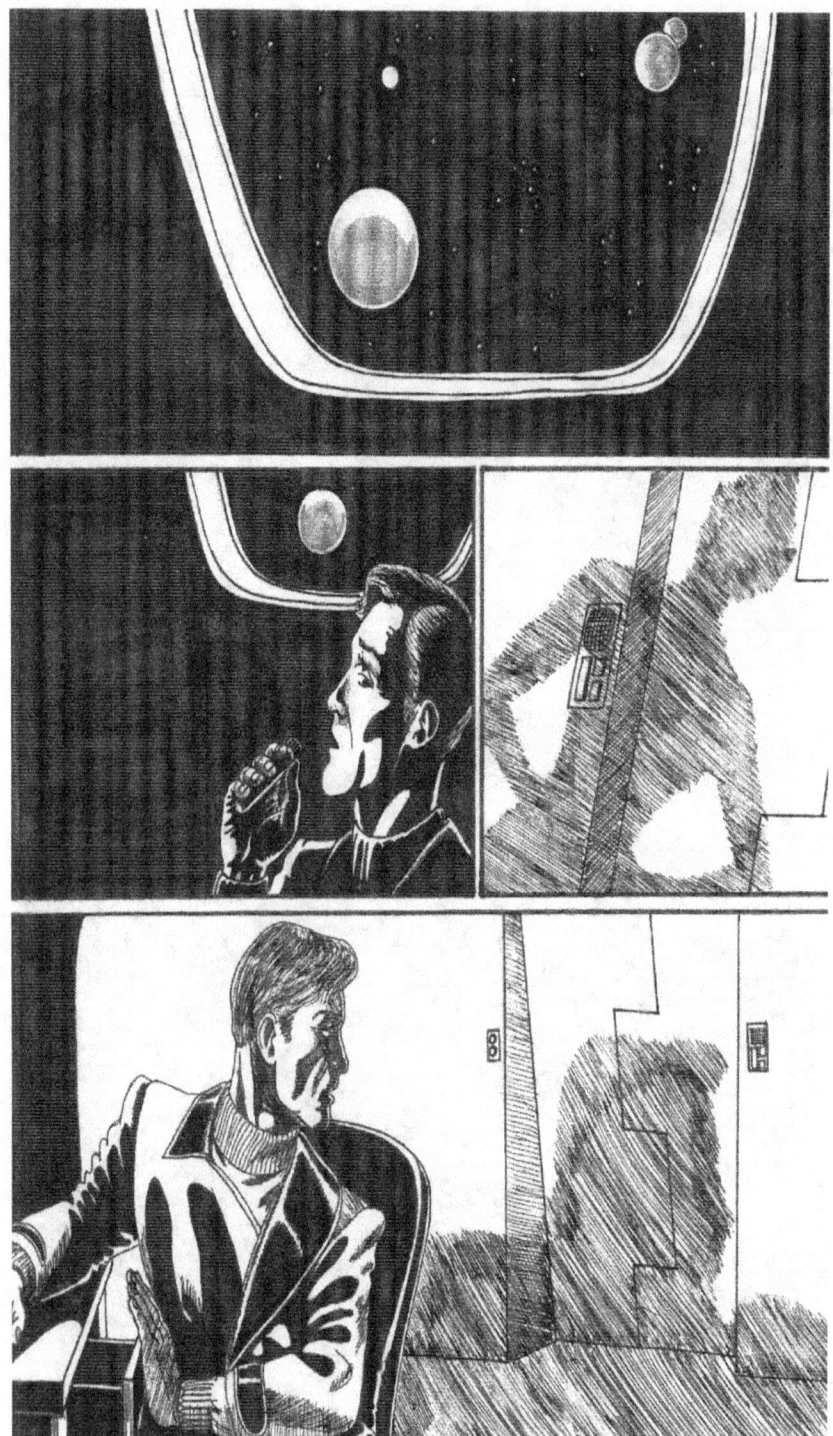

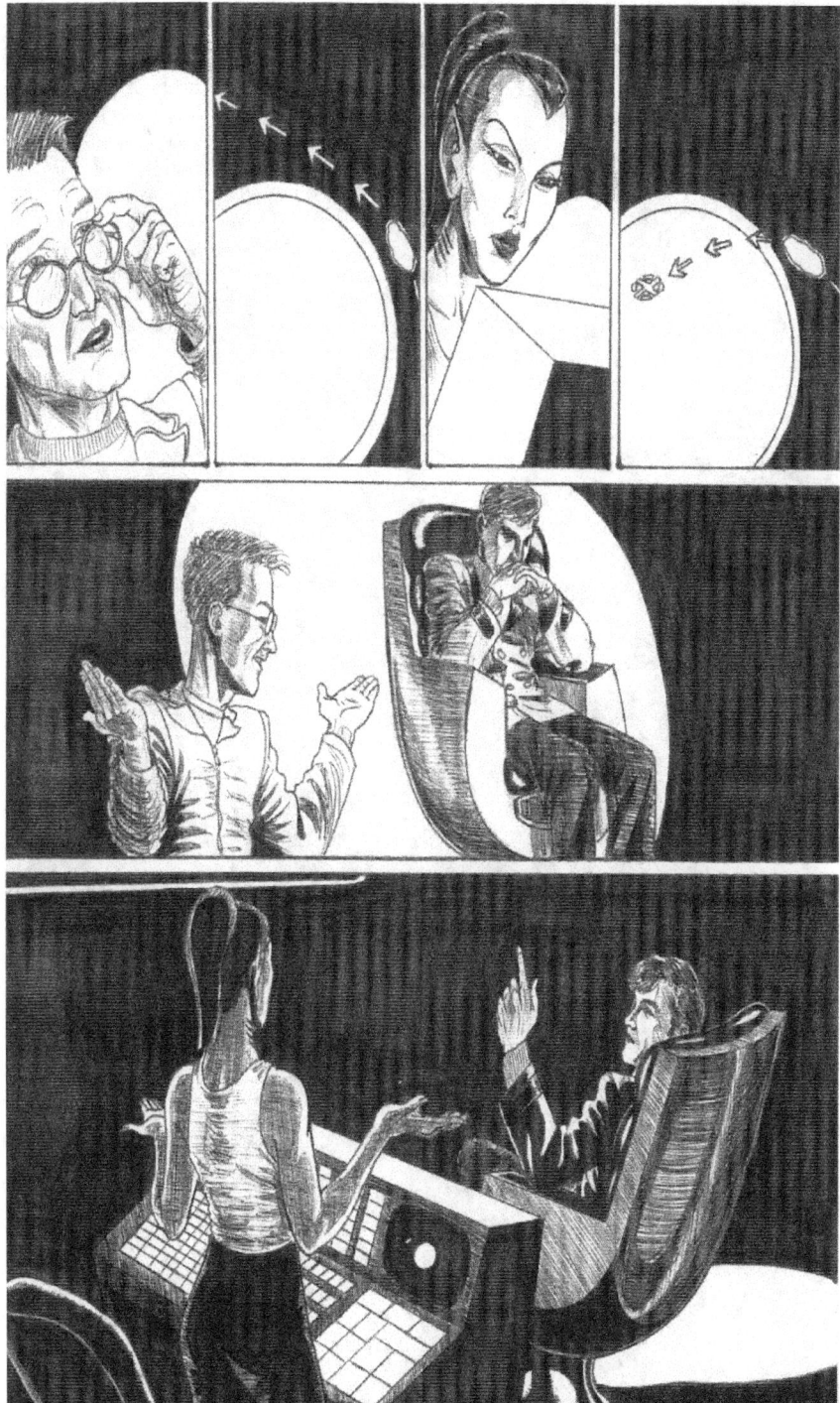

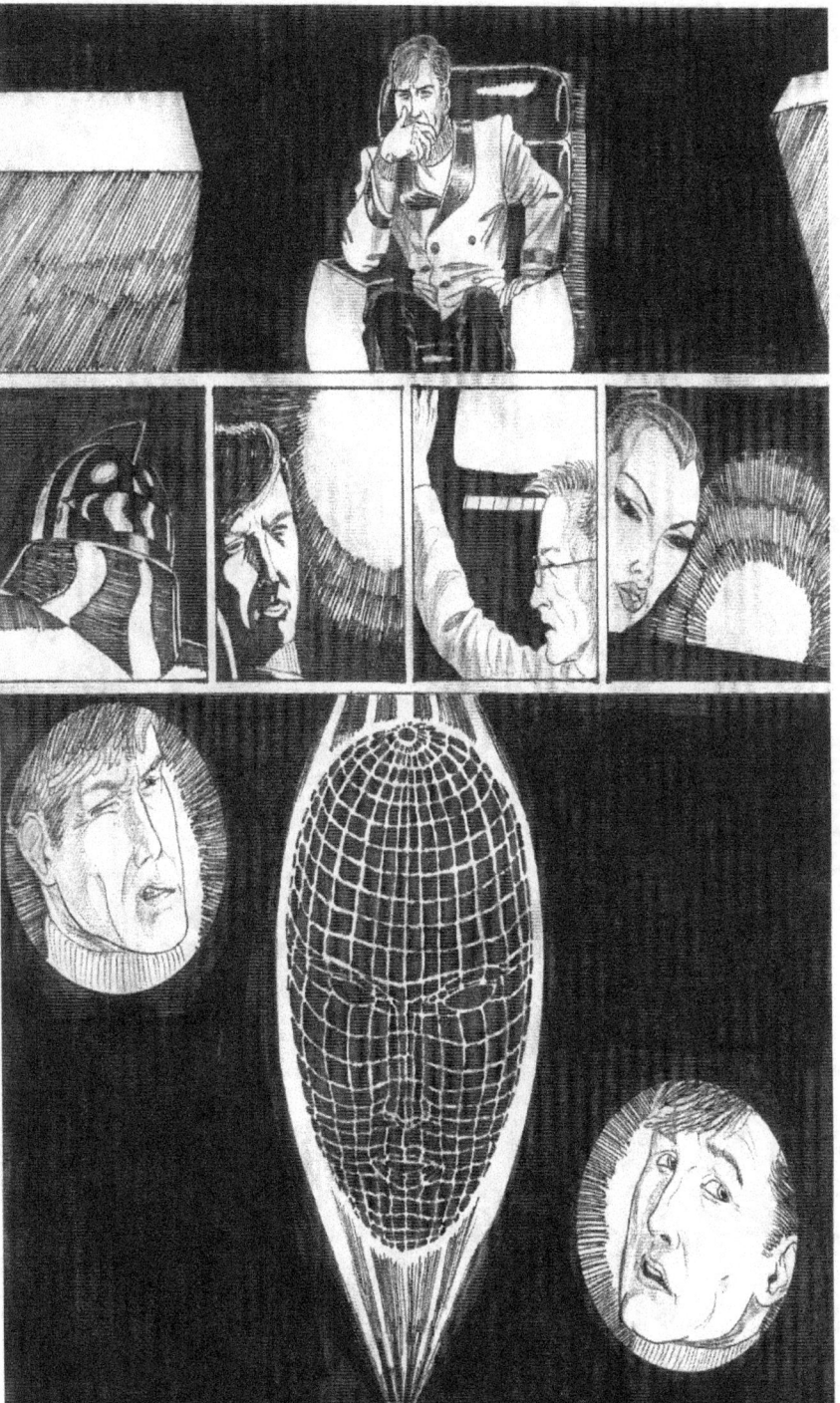

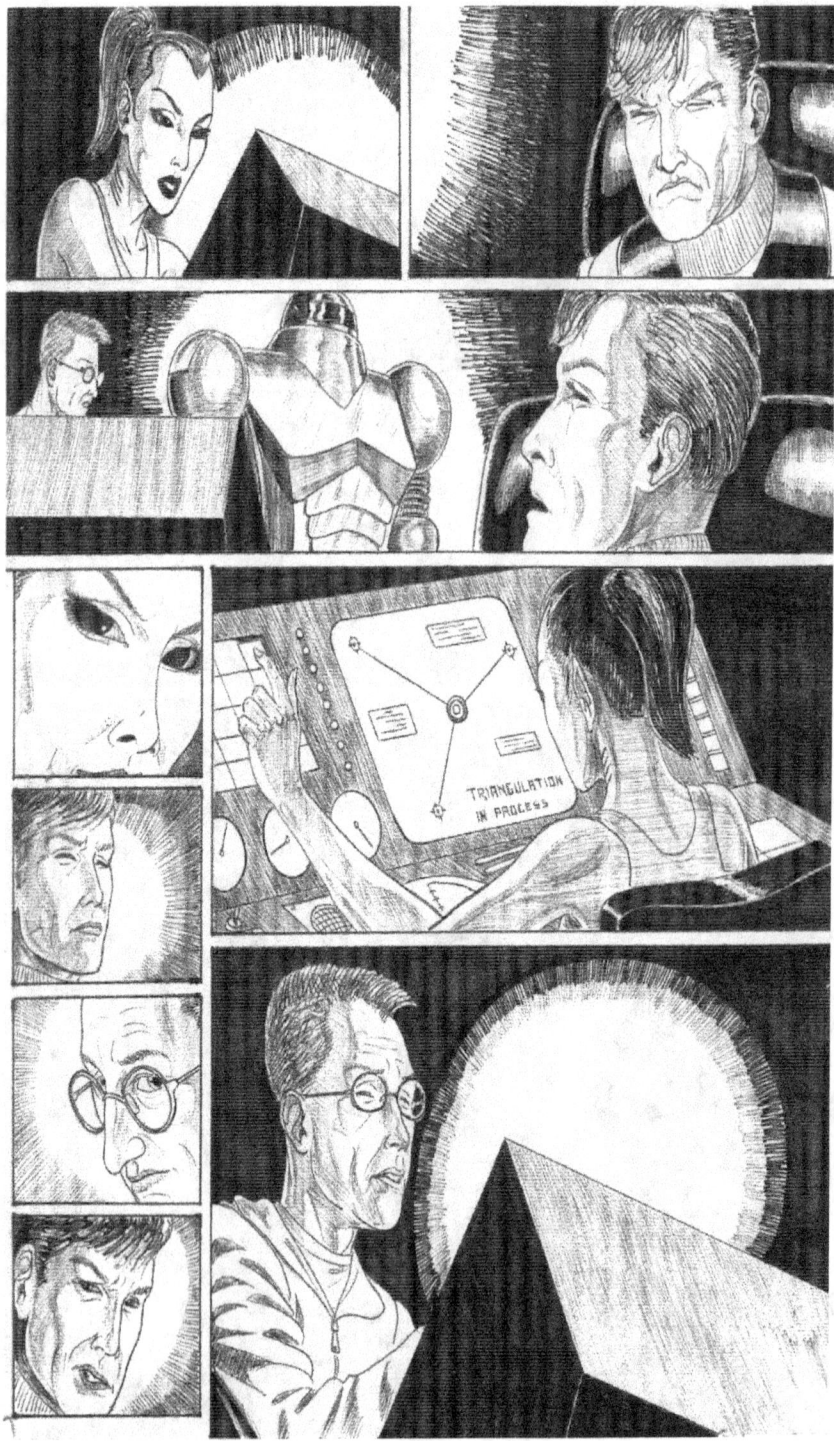

Pre-Production Sketches

These sketches were done by Steve Newton to help pitch the Swindlers film project to investors, production companies, filmmakers, and actors.

A look at an exasperated Bob speaking with the holographic representation of the ship's computer.

Bob gets a briefing from his crew about the asteroid.

This was the first sketch of the ship's bridge.

Watto, with his sister Dani, tries to give TK-421 a token of friendship.

Bob works his charms on Vina while admiring the view from the palace balcony.

Jana discusses her adventurous life with Ruafo

The Girellian High Council meets in the palace

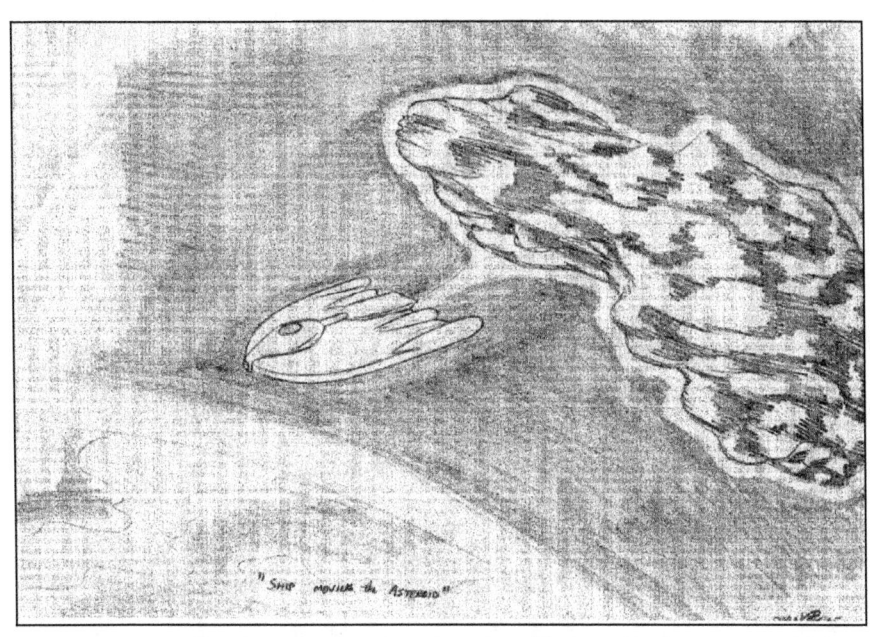

The ship attempting to maneuver the asteroid out of its collision course

Bob recording his memoirs in his cabin

Easter Eggs

This story was born from my love of all things Sci-Fi. I use "Sci-Fi" instead of "Science Fiction" because, for me at least, "Sci-Fi" evokes a fun, playful, not-so-serious take on the genre. It's Space Opera and rayguns, jetpacks and laser swords, aliens and dogfights with cities in the clouds and danger around every turn. It's *Buck Rogers in the 25th Century* and Flash Gordon, space hero AND quarterback for the N.Y. Jets.

When I started writing the first draft of Swindlers, I decided to throw in as many references to everything I love about the genre. There are Easter Eggs aplenty to be found in the 120 pages of the final draft. Here is a list of the conscious ones I hid for you to seek and find. Some are more obvious than others. How many did you pick up on?

Character Names: Many of the character names are knowing nods to *Star Trek* and *Star Wars* among other influences.

Vina is named after the character played by Susan Oliver in "The Cage", *Star Trek's* original pilot episode which starred Jeffrey Hunter as Capt. Pike. (Who could forget when the Talosians turned her into an Orion Slave Girl so she could seduce Capt. Pike?)

Ruafo's name is taken from the villain of *Star Trek: Insurrection*, played by the awesome F. Murray Abraham.

The wardroid designation for *TK-421* is taken from the

stormtrooper who was assigned to guard the Millennium Falcon in *Star Wars*. ("TK-421, why aren't you at your post?") Also, he refers to himself as an "Achilles 9000 series wardroid" which combines my love of Greek mythology and the HAL 9000 from *2001: A Space Odyssey*.

There are two character names that might seem like Easter Eggs or Sci-Fi references, but they were not planned to be. Swindlers was written in early 1999 and broadcast that summer. Imagine my surprise when I sat in a theater to see *Star Wars: The Phantom Menace* and found out that **Watto** was the name of Anakin and Shmi Skywalker's surly, junk dealing owner! George Lucas and I both spontaneously came up with the exact same character name out of thin air!

The other character name is **Mal Fecks**. Most people assume I chose the name Mal because of Joss Whedon's amazingly fantastic Space Western, *Firefly/Serenity*. For years (15 and counting to be exact,) I have had to deal with the similarities between Firefly and Swindlers. Usually, I just throw up my hands and say "Mine has aliens and robots!" But, just like finding out George Lucas used the name Watto at the same time I did, it was a strange feeling when I sat down on September 20, 2002 to see what the guy who did Buffy the Vampire Slayer was going to do with his Wild West and Spaceships mashup. When the premiere episode was over, I clearly remember looking at my then-girlfriend and saying, "That guy just did Swindlers." It looked like Swindlers, the characters sounded like mine, and the tone was spot on with my Sci-Fi tale. Damn that Joss Whedon! Then again...he didn't use aliens or robots or a talking computer. So, I one-upped him there. But, for the record, Mal Fecks was not named for Mal Reynolds. His name was meant to show he was a malcontent. Swindlers came before the Serenity and her crew launched. So, no chance for *Firefly* references. Maybe I'll have to find a way in the sequels...

While not named as a tip of the cap to another character, Jana Korel is described as aquatic and was inspired, in part, by Abe Sapien from Mike Mignola's *Hellboy* series.

One last character note...the Ship is never referred to by name. Her personality is definitely meant to pay homage to Nell, the ship flown by young Shad in *Battle Beyond the Stars*. However, I didn't want to go too far with the homage and just couldn't come up with a suitable name for Bob's vessel. So, she was stuck with being "The Ship" or "The Computer." So, for those wondering, the ship never had a name at any point of the writing or recording process.

Page One: Bob's opening voice over is definitely meant to be the stereotypical "Captain's Log" and begins just as *Star Trek*'s famous opening credits with "Space..." before sarcastically mocking the "Final Frontier." It was my intention for this opening monologue from Bob to set the tone of our story and put fans on notice that it wouldn't be the typical portrayal of good guys saving the universe.

Page Seven: The Iotian Precepts were inspired by *Star Trek: Deep Space Nine*'s Ferengi Rules of Acquisition. I liked the idea of a collection of fortune cookie wisdom which can be interpreted in different ways depending on your perspective or world view.

Page Thirteen: The first of many references to the UFP or the Federation...a tip of the cap to *Star Trek's* United Federation of Planets. Although, several dates mentioned during the course of the story do not match up with Star Trek history. So, this may not be the actual Trek Federation, after all...

Page Seventeen, Eighteen, and Twenty-One: Mal echoes several lines from Han Solo ("She'll hold together"), Montgomery Scott ("I'm giving it all she's got"), and James T. Kirk ("We need warp speed in three seconds or we're all dead".)

Page Twenty-Seven: The discussion about Vermicious Knids refers to an animal mentioned in Roald Dahl's *Charlie and the Chocolate Factory* which was made into one of my favorite childhood movies starring Gene Wilder as Willy Wonka. (Don't even get me started on the Tim Burton/Johnny Depp fiasco.)

Page Twenty-Nine: Puraso mentions life on the third planet in their star system. Hmmmm. Wonder what planet that could be...Also on this page, Ruafo's initial interactions with the council were meant to be similar to James Spader's performance as Daniel Jackson in the film version of *Stargate*.

Page Thirty-Six: Bob brings up an incident on the planet Malmori.

The Malmori were the bad guys lead by John Saxon's evil Sador in *Battle Beyond the Stars*.

Page Thirty-Eight: Bob's order for Jana to keep nodding as if he were giving orders is reminiscent of the same order from Kirk to Spock while stalling Khan for more time in *Star Trek II*.

Page Forty-Nine and Fifty: TK-421's adamantium tank treads and vibranium-alloy armor plating make the robot nearly invulnerable. Adamantium and Vibranium come from Marvel Comics with the former used to forge Wolverine's unbreakable skeleton and claws and the latter forming Captain America's impenetrable shield.

Also on Page Fifty, TK says he is from "Starhawk platoon Gamma." Starhawk is a Marvel Comics superhero who was part of the original Guardians of the Galaxy and fought alongside the Avengers in their battle with the powerful Korvac.

Page Fifty-Six: Not a Sci-Fi reference, but Puraso says many of the palace sculptures came from the Lost City of Bilagio Natte. While a SF tale, Swindlers is also a story about con men pulling off a heist a la *Ocean's Eleven* (which is one of my all-time favorite movies.) In this first Ocean movie, Danny Ocean and his team conspire to rob three Las Vegas casinos in one night. The casinos were the Mirage, the MGM Grand, and…the Bellagio.

Also, he mentions a "Galen the Second" which is a double Easter Egg as it refers to both the chimpanzee character played by Roddy McDowell in the original *Planet of the Apes* film as well as the Technomage Galen from the *Babylon 5* universe.

Page Fifty-Nine and Sixty: Bob explains how the crew plans on moving the asteroid out of the collision course with Girellia. His demonstration and identification of the tactics as the "Coyote Thrust Manuever" are from the asteroid-hurtling-towards-the-Earth epic *Armageddon* which may have been Michael Bay's last good movie. (Don't judge me. It's a fun movie!)

Page Eighty-One: Mal's line "The mains are bypassed like a Christmas tree. So, don't give me too many bumps" is another Scotty line from *Star Trek II*.

Page Eighty-Nine: TK-421's "Prime Directives" are an allusion to both the Federation's Prime Directive of non-interference in developing cultures in *Star Trek* as well as The Three Laws of Robotics created by Isaac Asimov and featured in his work *I, Robot*. TK's Directive Delta is based on the first of the three Asimov laws.

Page Ninety-Seven: Bob's reaction ("I love this plan. I'm glad to be a part of it.") to their plan to save Girellia is similar to that of Peter Venkman during the conclusion of *Ghostbusters*.

Page One Hundred: "Well, Bob, this is certainly a fine mess you've gotten yourself into." This line obviously harkens back to the great comedy duo of Stan Laurel and Oliver Hardy.

Surprisingly, considering all of the winks, nods, and tips of the cap I inserted into the story, this is the first published work of fiction I have written that doesn't have a reference to my all-time favorite movie, *Jaws*. Something I will have to rectify in the sequel…

Storyboards

The following storyboards were created by Eric Borchert for the climactic attempt to destroy the asteroid and rescue of Captain Bob as well as the opening sequence.

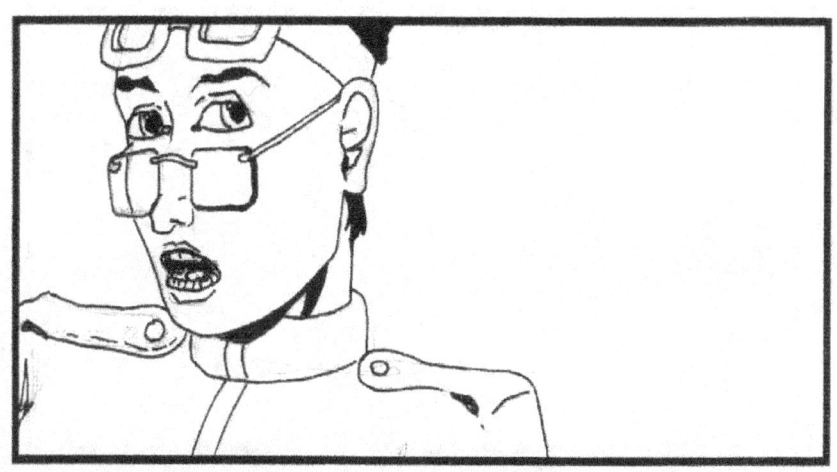

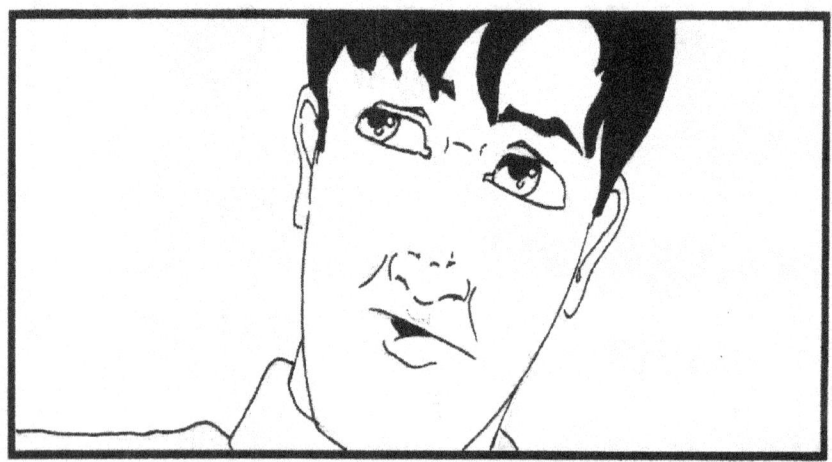

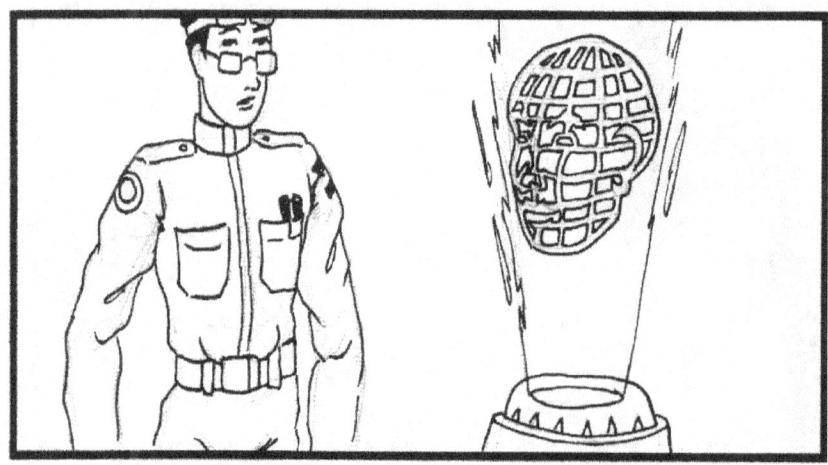

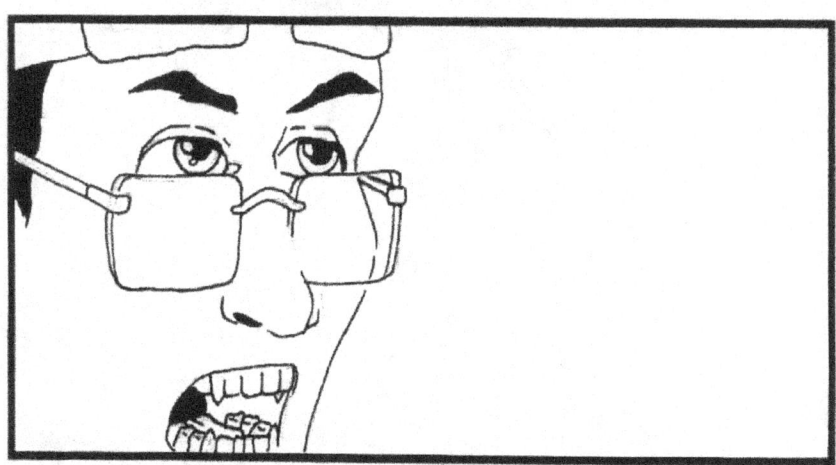

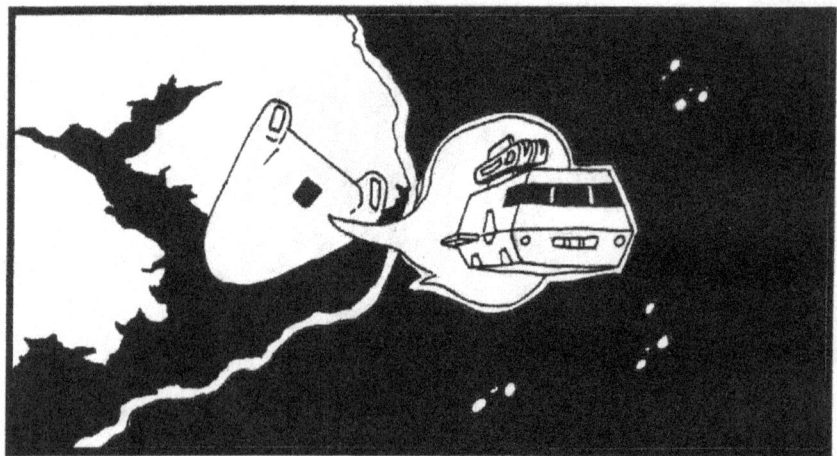

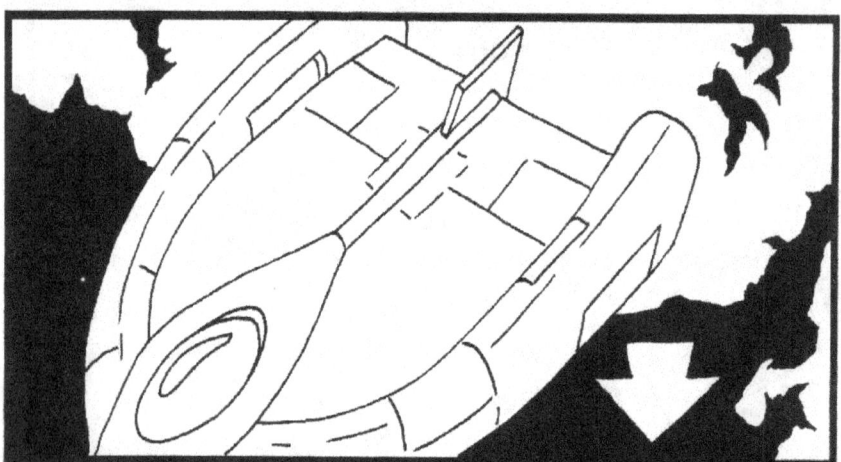

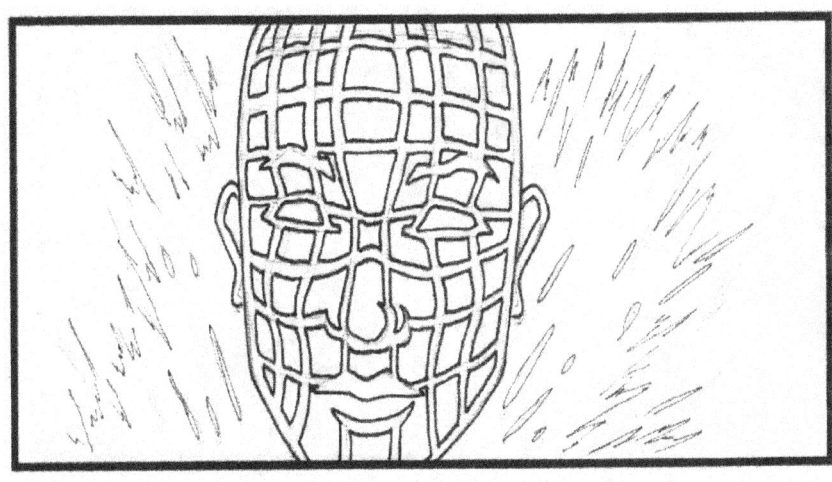

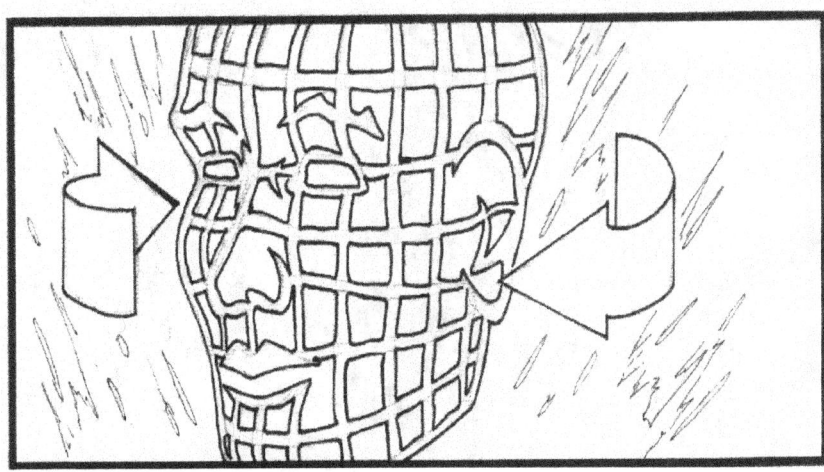

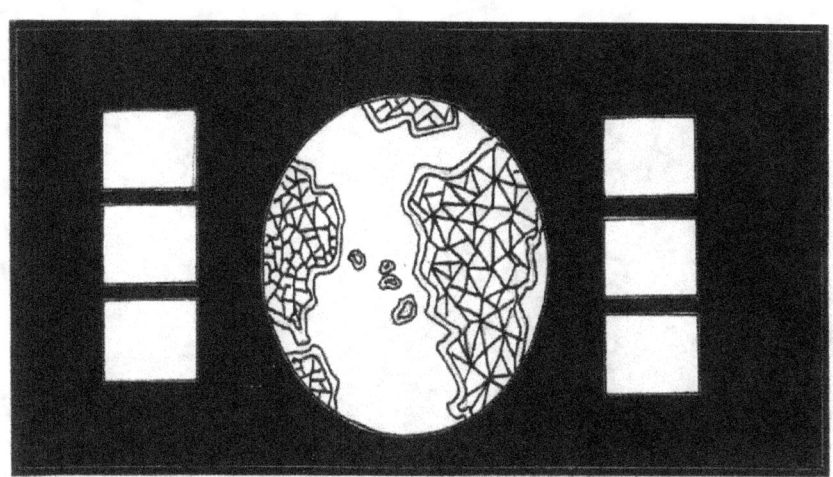

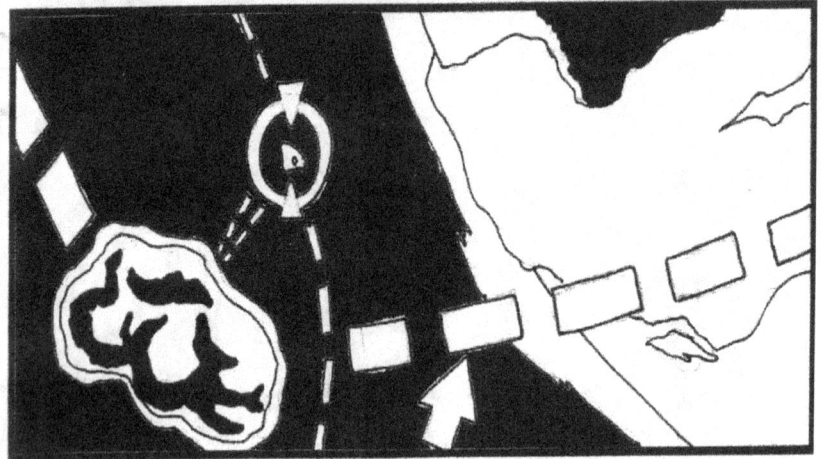
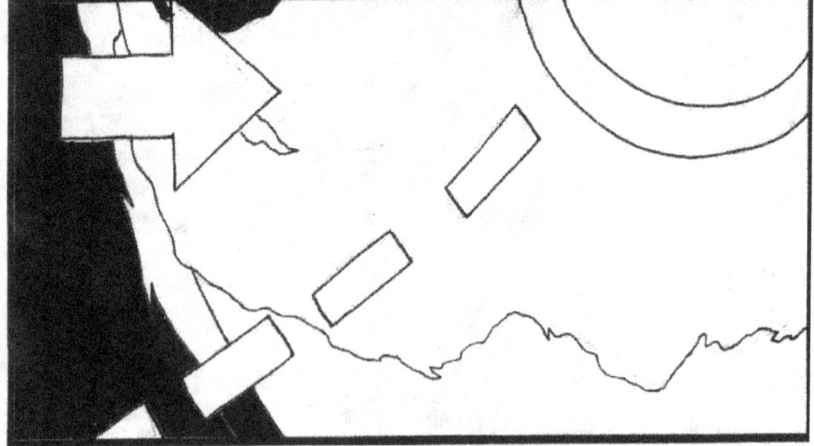

Character Sketches

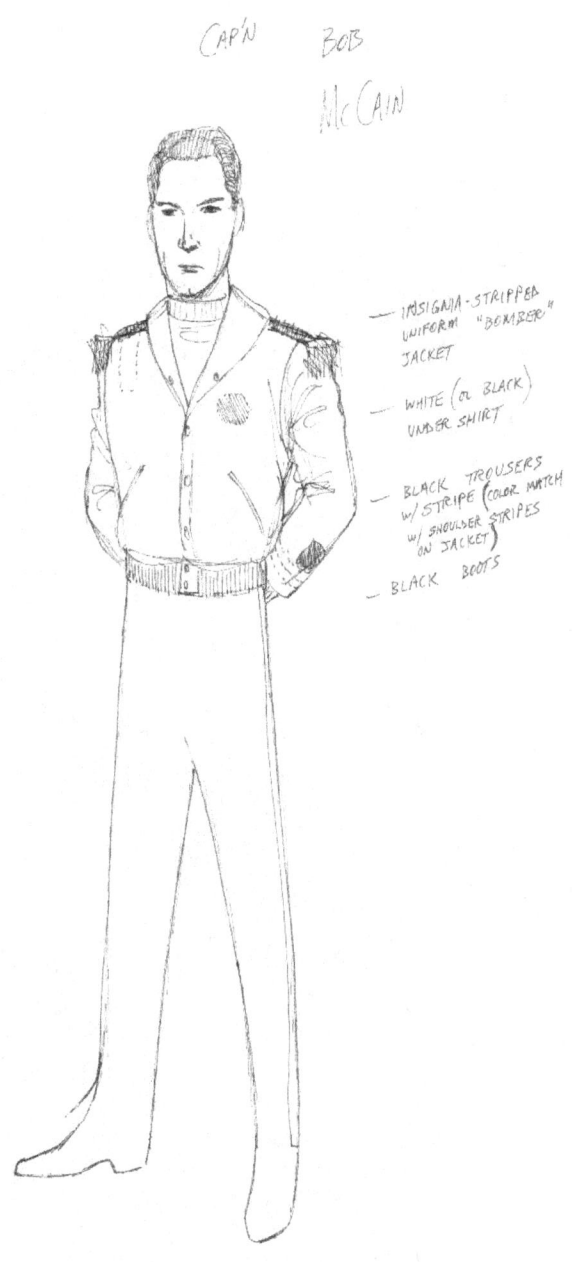

CAP'N BOB McCAIN

— INSIGNIA-STRIPPED UNIFORM "BOMBER" JACKET

— WHITE (OR BLACK) UNDER SHIRT

— BLACK TROUSERS W/ STRIPE (COLOR MATCH W/ SHOULDER STRIPES ON JACKET)

— BLACK BOOTS

Bob McCain as Your Ship's "Captain"

MAL FECKS
(ENGINEER)

— HEAVY-DUTY, MULTI-POCKETED
  MECHANICS-STYLE COVERALLS
  (~~BLUE~~ NEUTRAL GRAY)

— BLACK/WHITE UNDERSHIRT

— BLACK BOOTS

Mal Fecks as Your Ship's Engineer

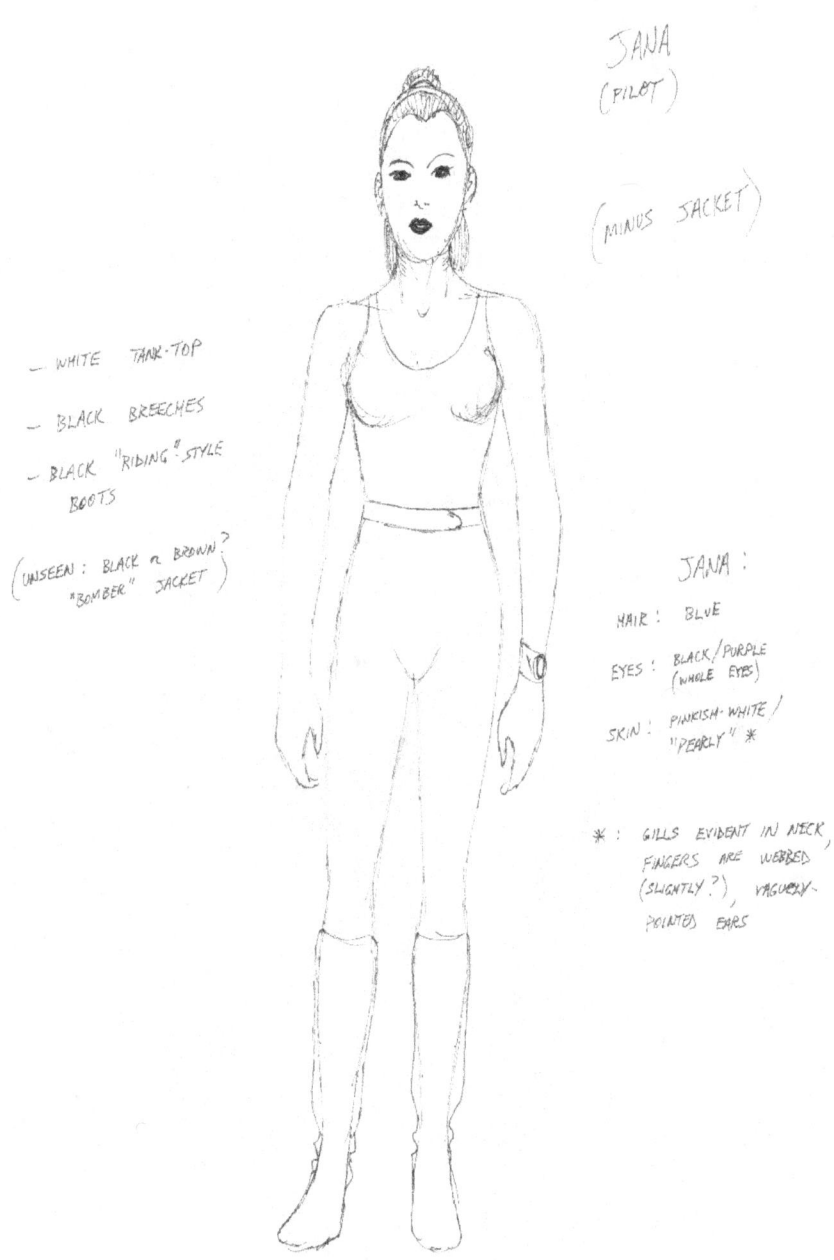

JANA
(PILOT)

(MINUS JACKET)

— WHITE TANK-TOP

— BLACK BREECHES

— BLACK "RIDING"-STYLE
    BOOTS

(UNSEEN: BLACK n BROWN?
    "BOMBER" JACKET)

JANA :

HAIR : BLUE

EYES : BLACK/PURPLE
       (WHOLE EYES)

SKIN : PINKISH-WHITE/
       "PEARLY" *

* : GILLS EVIDENT IN NECK,
    FINGERS ARE WEBBED
    (SLIGHTLY ?), VAGUELY-
    POINTED EARS

Jana Korel as Your Ship's Pilot

A Close Up of Jana showcasing her gill slits and other amphibian features

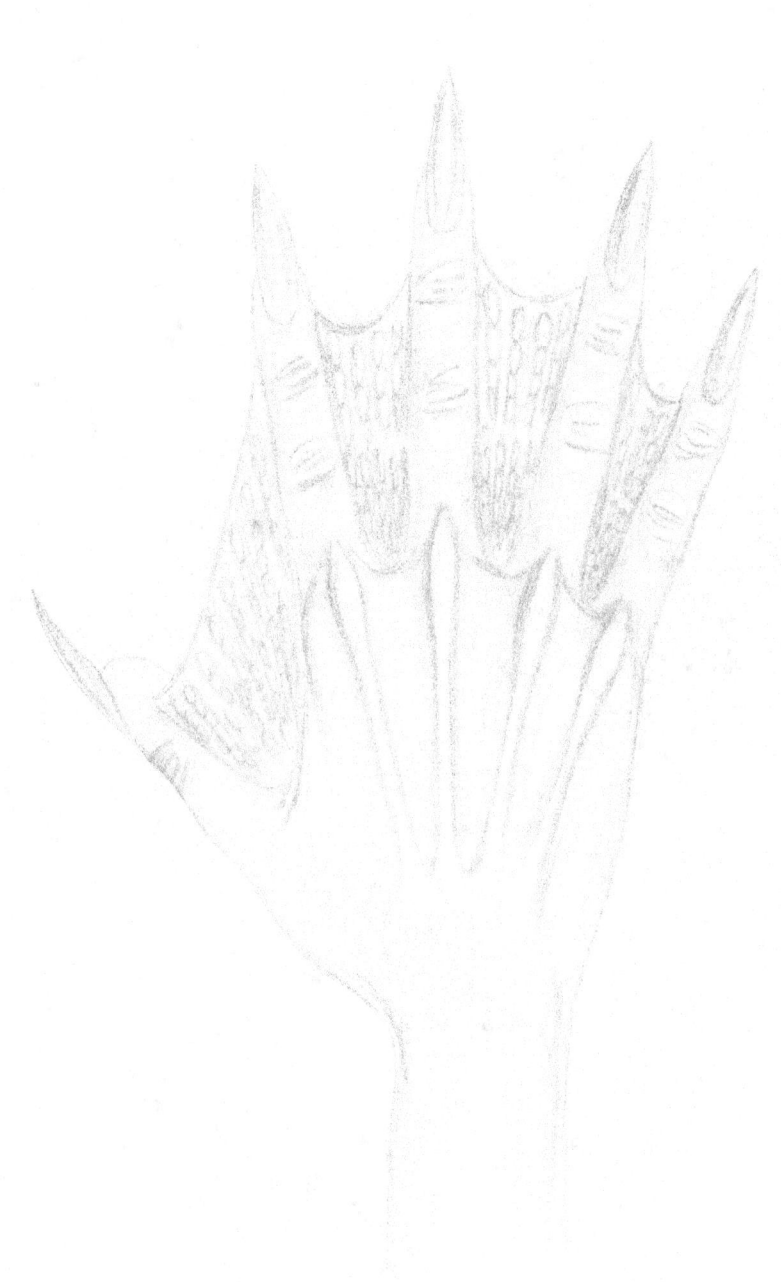

Jana's Webbed Hands

An early concept for TK-421

The Ship Designs

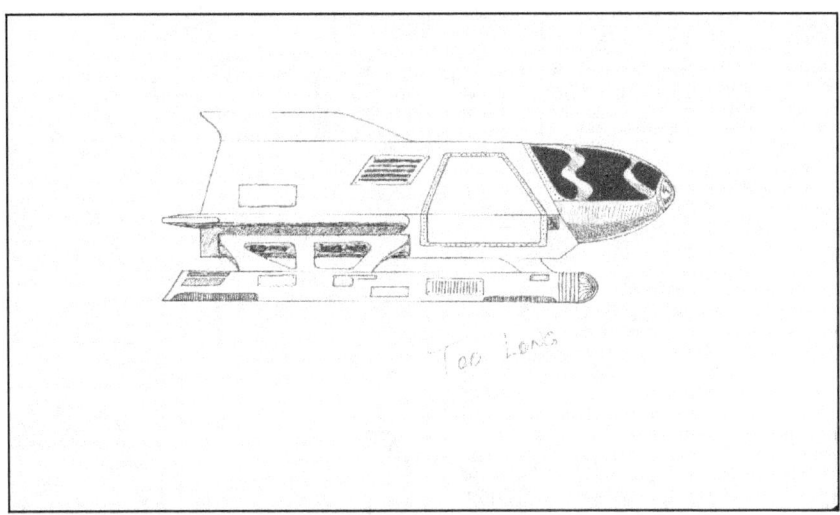

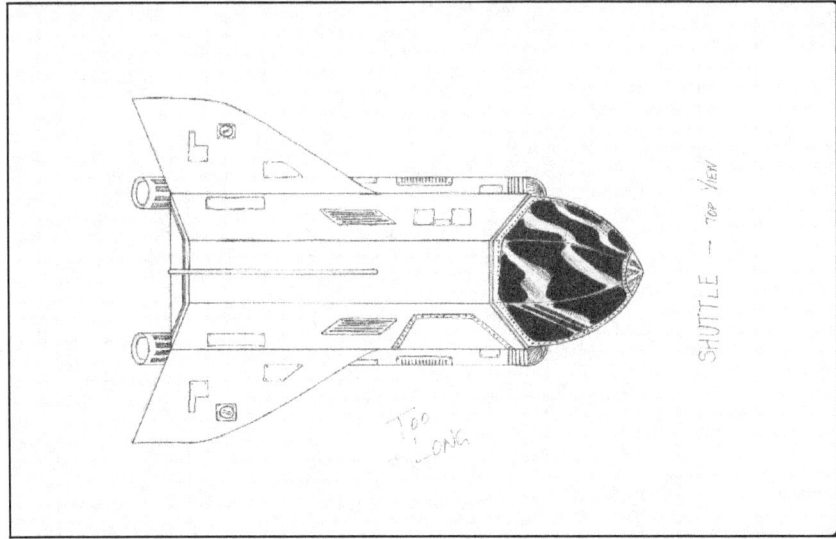

The penultimate shuttle design, including notes indicating one final change to shorten the craft's final look. A planned easter egg would have had faded markings indicating the shuttle's former name was "Galileo" after one of the more famous Star Trek shuttlecraft.

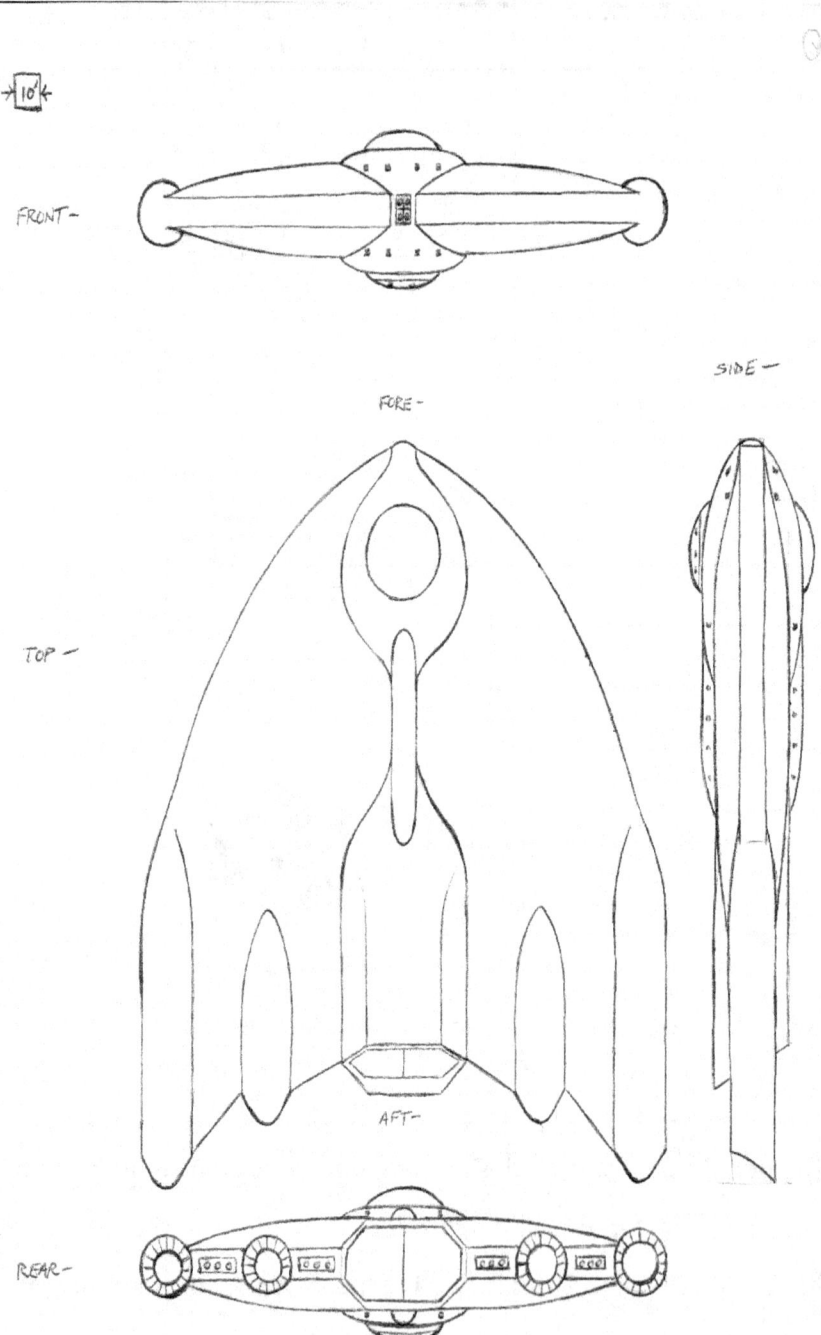

FRONT—

FORE—

SIDE—

TOP—

AFT—

REAR—

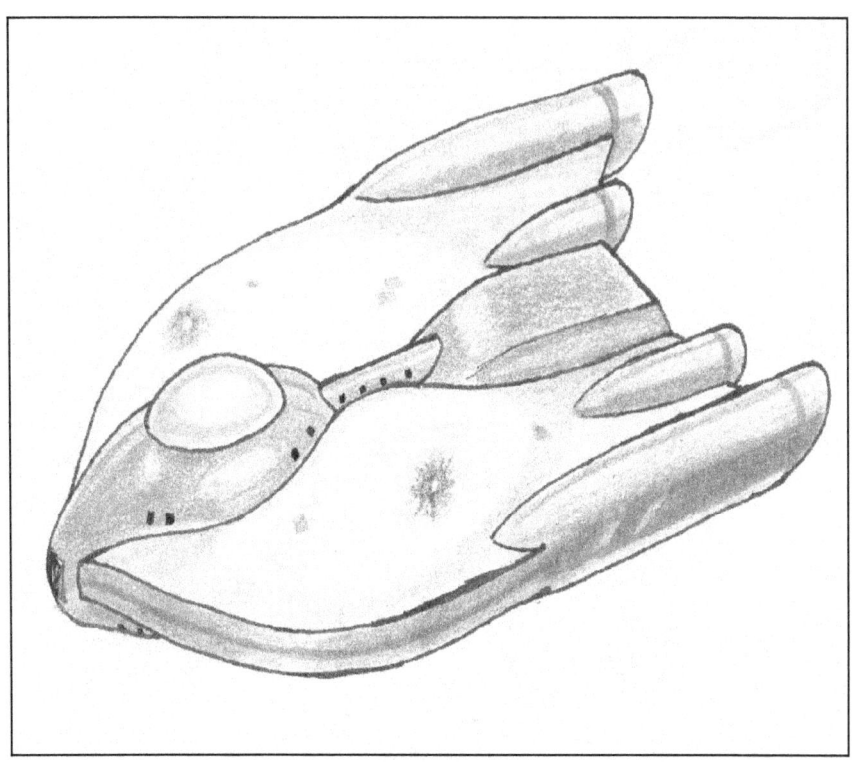

Although not revealed within the initial story, the idea was that this was a ship with some history. Probably floating around some futuristic junkyard or surplus depot after decades of service, how Bob acquired the vessel is still a mystery (even to this humble author.) Gut feelings lean towards Bob buying it at a surplus auction when he realized he needed a ship to help with his scheming. Or maybe he conned some low-level officer into releasing the rust bucket to him. However, one possible answer is not on the table...that Bob stole the ship. Stealing a starship is something I knew had to be saved for a Swindlers sequel so our crew could have a shiny, new ship.

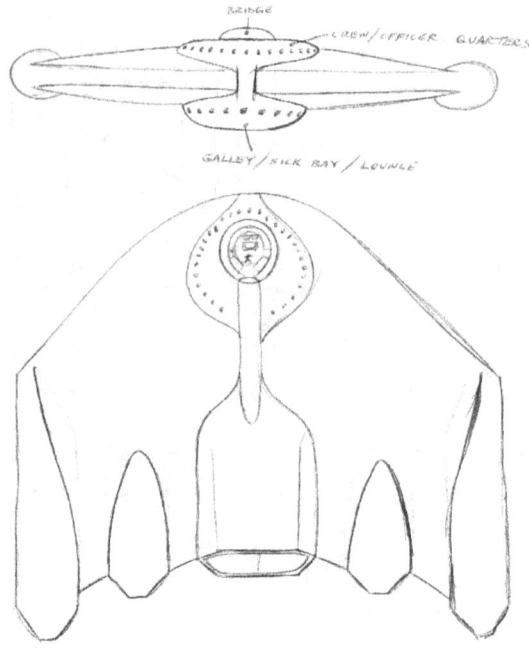

The Ship's Exterior.

The design incorporates ideas from such varied places as the

original Star Trek and movies like Forbidden Planet

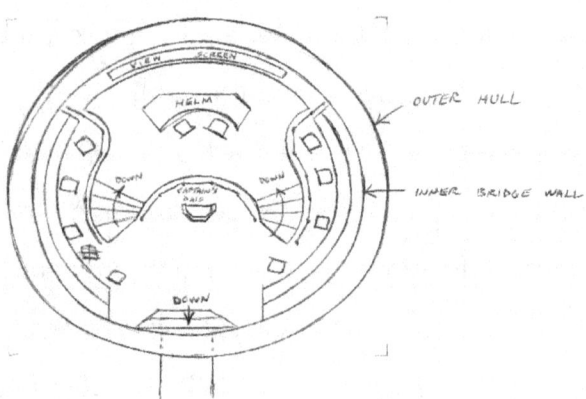

The layout for the Ship's Command Bridge.

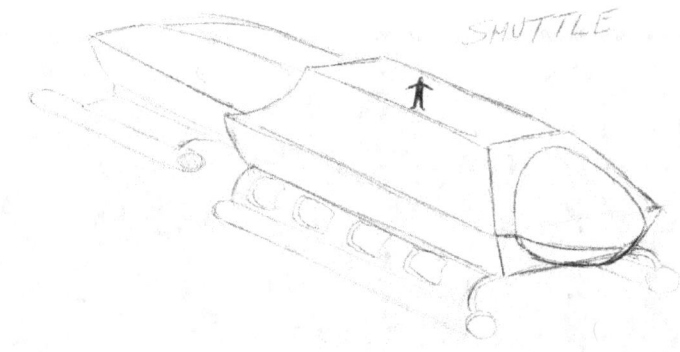

SHUTTLE

CARGO   PASSENGER COMPARTMENT   COCKPIT   12'

12'

30'

Some Early Sketches of the Crew's Shuttle

Pulp Fiction???

A pretty awesome pulp-style cover created using the Pulp-O-Mizer.

If only we had created Swindlers 60 years earlier...

SPECIAL THANKS TO:

The Original Swindlers Crew: Curt, Chris, Katie, Wayne, Debbie, Christy, Brian, Mikki, and especially the dearly departed Willy for signing up and bringing this story to life in ways I couldn't imagine

Kelli Lerner for being the first industry-type to believe in this story...one of these days we'll give it another shot

Jim Sr. and Barbara Yelton for understanding and feeding my love of all things sci-fi

KOPN Radio for taking a chance on the crazy idea of producing new, original radio dramas

Patrick Voss and Lloyd Longsworth for your support and excitement about this project

Mike Chronister for all of those childhood adventures...thanks for letting me be your Han Solo

Eric Stanze, Sandy Collora, Van Plexico, and so many others who are inspiring examples of being creative and pursuing your dreams...these people push me directly and indirectly to keep building worlds and creating adventures

Michelle Zellich and Fred & Stephania Grimm...Convention organizers who, years ago, made a huge impact on me in ways I can never repay...Thanks for not being too "Big Time" (or condescending as other Con Organizers can be) and making an honest effort to treat a newbie author like he was a pro

Enjoy a Sneak Preview of

MIDNIGHT ENTERTAINMENT'S

Exciting, Dramatic, New Superhero Series…

Coming in the Spring of 2015

EXTRA

ORDINARY

SEASON ONE

EPISODE ONE :

THE NEVERENDING BATTLE

From Jim Yelton & Steve Newton,

the creative talents who brought you

Alarm buzzers sounded and red emergency lights flashed along the instrument panel. The passenger jet's pilot did what he could to stabilize the aircraft while his co-pilot began speaking over the radio.

"This is Oceanic Flight 616. We are two hundred miles due east of Miami on a course heading of two-seven-zero. We have lost power and are unable to restart our engines," he said into his headset, "Our altitude is twenty four thousand feet and we are descending fast. Repeating...this is Oceanic..."

A small explosion rocked the cabin and they could see flames whipping along the wing outside the starboard windows.

In the passenger cabin, another jolt of turbulence startled the already panic stricken travelers. The flight attendants made their way up and down the aisle to comfort their charges and make sure everyone was following the emergency procedures.

One businessman near the front told his seat mate across the aisle, "This is why I always read the safety instructions. As much as I fly, the odds were bound to catch up to me."

An elderly couple several rows back were holding hands and whispering to each other...a woman was trying to use her cell phone to leave a message with one last goodbye to her family...newlyweds on their honeymoon were crying and sharing one last kiss.

In the midst of the turmoil and sadness, a little girl kept struggling to look out one of the windows while her mother was trying to squirm her into an inflatable life jacket.

"But, Mom...I saw something out there. Right before the engine caught on fire," the curious girl argued.

Her frustrated mother closed the window shade and said, "You probably just saw whatever caused the fire or a piece of the wing flying off. For Pete's sakes, Alyssa, you need to pay attention. The captain said we need to be ready when he tries to land on the water."

Undeterred, Alyssa reopened the shade and pointed out the window, "It wasn't a piece of the wing or an explosion. I saw something out there coming flying toward us."

From the seat behind them, another passenger stuck his head up.

"I saw something, too," he said, "It might have just been a bird."

"Or another plane," an elderly woman offered from across the aisle.

Alyssa's Mother furrowed her brow and shot the others a "You're-not-helping" look of disapproval before turning back to her daughter.

"Just close the window and follow the attendant's instructions," Mother demanded.

"But, Mom...what if...?" Alyssa half-heartedly started.

The man behind them leaned forward and pointed out their window.

"Look!" he shouted.

Alyssa's mouth grew into a Cheshire grin and she said, "It's him. I told you."

A passing flight attendant, craning her neck to join other passengers looking out another window, cheered, "It's Golden Defender!"

They watched a flash of gold and white speed past the plane and the crowd's mood instantly changed from despair to hope. The World's Greatest Hero had arrived to save the day.

Outside of the plane, Golden Defender, slowed his flight near the cockpit windows and nodded to the pilot and co-pilot before speeding up again and flying to the nose of the plane.

The co-pilot began to update the ground, "Control, you're not going to believe this. Golden Defender just arrived. I think we're going to be Ok."

He smiled at the pilot and the two exchanged a look of relief just as another explosion shook the aircraft.

The pilot glanced back to the control panel and said, "We just lost number two. Defender got here just in time."

"Doesn't he always?" the co-pilot asked rhetorically.

Back in the passenger cabin, the passengers and flight attendants were all trying to look out any available window to catch a glimpse of their savior. Those who could not squeeze close enough to a window were cheering and hugging each other. Passengers with a better view watched Golden Defender settle underneath the nose of the jet and then reverse his course, slamming into the fuselage with a thud before his massive strength started to pull the plane from its fatal descent.

The hero needed all of his power to change the jet's course. Unfortunately, he couldn't hear the passengers cheering him on. Just the plane's engines fighting to keep them airborne, the wind whipping around him, and his own breathing getting a bit more labored. He focused his concentration and used his enhanced hearing to find out what the flight crew was up to.

He heard the pilot say, "We're leveling off. This is the captain speaking. We are leveling off. However, until we land safely, we need everyone to remain calm and in the emergency position. Everything is in the hands of Golden Defender..."

Golden Defender started to struggle slightly in his bid to slow down the plane. The strain became evident on his face and he began to dig his fingers into the fuselage as if it were aluminum foil, not steel. Turbulence caused him to lose his grip and the jet lurched as he slipped from its nose and fell past the wing before getting a grip on the tail section.

The tail rudder broke apart and the hero had to refocus his effort on flying back up to the nose section. As he swooshed past them, he noticed the worried passengers looking out various windows as he sped toward the front of the plane.

A shudder ran through the cabin as the passengers felt the impact of Defender taking control of the plane again.

"It's fine..."

"He'll save us..."

"I can't believe it's really him..."

"Did you get a picture of him, Jimmy?"

Golden Defender started to make another attempt at slowing the plane safely. Sweat began to break out on his brow as he clenched the jet with all of the strength he could muster. It wasn't enough and the jet continued to free fall.

Defender struggled to tighten his grip and, under the sound of the wind rushing around him, he could hear another sound...the sound of his heart beating...faster and faster as a strange sensation set in...a sensation he had never felt before...Panic. Something was wrong and he felt powerless to stop it.

The nose of the jet crumbled under his hold and the mighty hero began to fall helplessly away from the jet. Defender saw one of the jet's wings break apart as he started spinning out of control in a free fall. He reached out one last time to summon whatever power he had left…trying to fly before succumbing to the reality that for… whatever reason… his powers were gone. His eyelids fluttered as he fought against the coming unconsciousness. However, he was powerless against that as well and the last thing he saw before passing out was the huge explosion filling the sky…

To Save the World, Ordinary Heroes Must Become

Extra Ordinary

It's time for 30 Minutes of Sci-Fi…

30 Minutes of Fantasy…

30 Minutes of Movies, TV, and Pop Culture…

Join host Jim Yelton & guests from across the

genre multiverse.

Get your Geek on 30 Minutes at a time!

Find it at www.midnight-entertainment.com or

www.thegeekspeaknetwork.net

About the Author

Jim Yelton has been creating in one way or another since his early teens. Starting in theater as an actor and becoming a director while still in high school, he has been involved in over 30 stage productions. Jim is an experienced radio talk show host and always found a way to sneak in his passion for movies and assorted geeky topics way before it was cool. But his real love has always been writing and Jim has written for various media including Radio Dramas, graphic novels, short stories, stage productions, and screenplays.

A child of the 70's and 80's, he has channeled his love of the two "Stars"-Trek and Wars, Marvel Comics, and horror movies into a variety of projects including founding Midnight Entertainment, writing the upcoming superhero illustrated novel series Extra Ordinary, and hosting the podcast 30 Minutes of Geek.

Very opinionated and knowledgeable about a wide variety of Pop Culture topics, Jim has been a convention panelist and podcast guest covering everything from Battlestar Galactica to his love of all things Buffy and Joss Whedon-y as well as workshops covering Screenwriting and Beating Writer's Block. He is also teaching Screenwriting and Novel Writing courses in the Mid-Missouri area and is turning his class lessons into an upcoming book entitled "Everything I Learned about Writing Came from Spider-Man, Star Trek, and a Shark Named Bruce."

Jim lives in Mid-Missouri with his wife, Sonya, and their two daughters, Andrea and Jamie.

About the Artists

Steve Newton longs for the glory days of classic pulp fiction when shadowy vigilantes and two-fisted heroes fought evil and traveled the world in search of adventure. An expert on all things Batman, Sherlock Holmes, and much more, he uses both his artistic and writing talents in a wide variety of media. He also claims to know what evil lurks in the hearts of men. Steve resides in St. Louis, MO, which provides him an opportunity to cheer on his beloved baseball Cardinals every summer.

Eric Borchert works as a graphic artist by day and is father to his wonderful daughter Melynda. In his free time, he enjoys using his artistic ability to give two dimensional life to superheroes, star warriors, and fantastic worlds. When he isn't being a father or artist, he can be found racing around Tennessee as an avid competitive runner. Eric and Melynda make their home in Columbia, TN.

www.ingramcontent.com/pod-product-compliance
Lightning Source LLC
Chambersburg PA
CBHW061222170626
46809CB00007B/2555